"You
to enjo

"You may be right."

"I'm always right."

She laughed. "I'll remember that."

"Are you too tired for more?"

"No way." She took his hand and followed him back onto the ice.

They skated hand in hand, and he twirled her around expertly before bringing her into a pair spin at such a high rate of speed that she was dizzy when they stopped. She leaned into his hard body for balance. Her hands were pressed against his chest and his rested on her waist. They stared deeply into each other's eyes—each knowing they should move away, yet unable to do so. The smiles on their lips died.

Natasha's heart skipped several beats as she waited for Damien's next move. Never releasing her, his face moved closer to hers. One of his hands left her waist to cup her jaw, drawing her nearer. His thumb caressed her smooth cheek. They gravitated together centimeter by centimeter until their lips touched lightly in butterfly kisses at first, but then the dam quickly broke and his mouth demanded and hers surrendered.

They quickly forgot everyone around them and lost themselves in each other.

Books by Judy Lynn Hubbard

Kimani Romance

These Arms of Mine
Our First Dance

JUDY LYNN HUBBARD

is a native of Dallas, Texas, and has always been an avid reader—particularly of romance. Judy enjoys well-written, engaging stories with characters she can identify with, empathize with and root for. Judy believes reading and writing are emotional experiences. She loves to write and her goal is to leave each reader completely satisfied when they finish one of her books. When writing, she honestly can't wait to see what happens next; she knows if she feels that way, she's created characters and a story that readers will thoroughly enjoy—and that's her ultimate goal.

Our First
DANCE

JUDY LYNN HUBBARD

KIMANI
ROMANCE

To my sister, Norma,
who instilled in me a love of reading,
and to my cousin and best friend, Trina, who instilled
in me a love of the arts. Thanks for believing in me.

Recycling programs
for this product may
not exist in your area.

ISBN-13: 978-0-373-86267-2

OUR FIRST DANCE

Copyright © 2012 by Judy Lynn Hubbard

Dear Reader,

I've always loved the grace and beauty of the ballet, so it's natural I would write a book about it.

My original plan was to write a reunion romance about a ballerina (Natasha Carter) who had chosen her career over her true love (Damien Johnson); however, through the collaborative editing process, the story evolved into a tale of two people brought together by chance, who grow to know, like and eventually love each other.

I hope you enjoy Natasha and Damien's journey to true love as much as I enjoyed writing it.

As I completed *Our First Dance*, a sequel featuring Marcy and Nathan (Natasha and Damien's siblings) began running rampant through my mind—so, I think I'll have to tell their story soon.

Watch my website for further news and, in the meantime, curl up with *Our First Dance* and enjoy!

Judy Lynn Hubbard

www.JudyLynnHubbard.com

Chapter 1

Natasha Carter's slender frame huddled deeper into her black leather jacket against the brisk mid-September wind, feet hurriedly walking through downtown Manhattan on the way to the most important audition of her career. How many lead auditions had she gone to in the past frustrating years only to come away disappointed? She sighed audibly. She had been surprised and thrilled upon receiving an invitation from the Johnson Ballet Company to try out for the part of Juliet. She was determined things would be different this time.

Shivering, she continued resolutely toward what she hoped would be a turning point in her career. She had to have the part of Juliet! She was tired of being cast in secondary roles or as part of the background dancers because she "wasn't quite right" for the lead. She deserved her chance in the spotlight, but up until now, no one had been willing to take a chance on her, an African-American ballerina.

Also, because she came from a wealthy family, no one took her dedication and drive seriously—believing instead she was merely *toying* with a career in dance.

Glancing both ways, she hurriedly crossed the busy street and entered the performance hall building she had been trying to reach for the past thirty minutes. A grateful smile perked up the corners of her brown lips as the blessed warmth inside greeted her. She looked at the signs that pointed the way to the auditions. Taking off her leather gloves, she stuffed them into her jacket pockets and absently ran fingers through her wind-tossed, shoulder-length dark brown hair before tucking strands behind her ears.

She nodded curt hellos to several fellow ballerinas as she entered the tryout hall to check in. For a moment she wished she had allowed Erina, her coach, to accompany her, but she had firmly dismissed her offer. She was a first-rate ballerina who didn't need anyone to hold her hand. She could and would do this alone, and she would come out victorious.

"May I help you?" A man behind the table was looking at her expectantly.

"Yes. I'm…"

"Natasha Carter." A woman smiled and stood.

She was tall and thin, obviously an ex-dancer. Her black hair was cut very short and framed her smiling face and happy brown eyes. She was, Natasha would guess, in her early forties.

"Yes." Natasha smiled slightly. It was nice to be recognized.

"We're so glad you could make the auditions, Miss Carter." The woman offered her hand. "I'm Rachel Weston. I'll be coproducing and codirecting this little extravaganza, along with taking on the responsibility of casting director."

"It's very nice to meet you, Ms. Weston." She briefly shook her hand.

"Rachel," she corrected.

Rachel's eyes traveled over Natasha. She looked perfect for the lead. But Rachel knew that looks alone were not enough for Damien. Over the years, she had learned how by the book and fanatical he was about his ballet company—only the best talent could work for him, no exceptions. She sighed inwardly as she recounted the numerous hours they had spent scouting for dancers to audition for them before sending out invitations; it had been exhausting, but Damien had insisted they personally sit through entire performances for every dancer being considered for his production.

"Room number three is set up for Miss Carter." Rachel walked from behind the desk. "Damien is around here somewhere." She glanced around the crowded room before refocusing on Natasha. "Let me show you to your dressing room."

"Thank you."

Natasha eagerly followed her out. Her heart somersaulted in her chest; she was in no shape to meet Damien Johnson yet. She needed a few moments to compose herself before coming face-to-face with the legendary owner of the company she hoped to join.

"I'll have someone call when we're ready for you." Rachel held open a door for her.

"Thank you, Ms. Weston." She smiled briefly while placing her bag onto the floor.

"Rachel," she reminded with a smile.

"Rachel," she said corrected and returned her smile.

Once alone, Natasha placed hands to her burning cheeks. She was a mass of quivering jelly. She silently commanded her nerves to subside and rolled her shoulders, shaking out her arms and legs to relax, but to no avail.

Damien Johnson was here! Of course, she had known he would be, but still the fact that her idol was somewhere in the same building was unreal. He was only thirty-two, but he owned one of the best ballet companies in the world. His meteoric rise had inspired her, and she clung to the hope that he would give her a chance where others had not; after receiving her invitation to audition for him, she felt certain that he would, but only if she performed flawlessly, which she intended to do.

She quickly shed her street shoes and sweats and donned much more appropriate prima ballerina attire of pale pink leotards, matching jagged-edge wraparound chiffon skirt belted at her tiny waist and expertly laced-up pale pink satin ballerina slippers. Finally, she pulled her hair away from her face, securing it at her nape in a flawless knot.

After taking a deep breath and releasing it slowly, she purposefully walked over to the ballet barre and began to warm up.

"Damien, there you are." Rachel reentered the audition hall and spotted her partner onstage.

A teasing grin lit up his brown eyes. "Was I lost?"

"Oh, you!" She laughed and tapped his cheek playfully. "Natasha Carter is here."

"Good, that makes everyone—" Damien rubbed his lightly hair-covered chin "—doesn't it?"

"Mmm-hmm," Rachel said and nodded.

"Okay, I have a few calls to make." He glanced at his watch. "We'll start in about thirty."

"Right," Rachel said with a nod. "I'm going to check the music." She turned and asked, "Do you want to do the introductions, or should I?"

Damien sighed. "You do them. The last thing I need today is a bunch of ballerinas fawning all over me thinking it will improve their chances of making the cut."

Rachel laughed. "You're just too handsome for your own good."

Damien chuckled. "Or just too rich and powerful."

He winked at Rachel before turning to go to his office. As he exited the auditorium, for some reason, his mind drifted to Natasha Carter's arrival a short while ago; she had breezed in looking breathtakingly beautiful. He knew the dark brown hair that had curtained her oval face would be swept up or back when he saw her next, and she would be dressed in classic ballerina attire—sheer, sexy leotards that would mold revealingly to her slender yet womanly curves like a second skin.

He had watched her from the stage as she had smiled politely to Rachel and had intended to join them, but his feet had been rooted in place by her utter beauty. He had mentally scolded himself to stop staring at her like some lovesick schoolboy; however, feelings he hadn't had in a long time had bombarded him, causing the formation of a hard knot of desire in the pit of his stomach.

Taking a deep breath and releasing it slowly, he attributed his reaction to the fact that she was an extremely beautiful woman, and as a man, he naturally took note of that fact. However, he was here to cast his ballet; she was here to audition, and he would objectively judge her by her performance and nothing else.

Thirty minutes later, the four auditioning ballerinas took the stage and waited for instructions. Rachel and Damien entered the back of the auditorium. Damien stopped at a pair of high stools a distance from the stage, and Rachel continued toward the stage to give instructions.

"Welcome, ladies." Rachel smiled at the four ballerinas as she ascended the stairs. "The Johnson Ballet Company is a world-renowned, medium-sized classical ballet company. We perform about sixty to seventy ballets a year in the U.S. and abroad. This holiday season, we are performing a traditional yet original version of *Romeo and Juliet*. You all know the order of your performances?" When she received nods, she continued, "Good. Let's have the first dancer, please."

Rachel smiled and nodded to her assistant to begin the taped music of Tchaikovsky's Symphony No. 4 before leaving the stage to join Damien. She took the packet of resumés he handed her and pulled out the first one.

The first ballerina walked center stage and danced adequately, as did the second and the third. Natasha was the last to dance. She assumed the fourth position, hands held elegantly at her sides, patiently waiting for the music to begin.

Natasha mentally fought for composure and concentrated with all her might on the dance at hand. Her heart had begun beating erratically the moment she had stepped onto the stage, because she knew this was the moment of truth for her. If she couldn't make it in a black-owned ballet company, then she wouldn't be able to make it anywhere, and that scenario was unacceptable to her.

Though she could no longer see Damien Johnson because of the bright light shining in her eyes, she knew the pair of piercing eyes she felt following every move, every line and curve her body made as she floated across the stage belonged to him. She silently willed herself to be perfect; she refused to allow nerves to destroy this chance for her. She beat down her anxiety and poured all her energy and talent into her performance.

A smile of admiration tugged at the corners of Damien's mouth as his appreciative eyes followed every seamless movement of Natasha's lithe body. He looked briefly at her resumé then looked at the stage. She danced ethereally.

Even at twenty-six, she danced circles around the five-to-eight-years-younger ballerinas who had come before her.

He watched with satisfaction as she performed a series of pirouettes and came effortlessly to a fast stop, holding and maintaining her ending position—back arched, arms held high, legs extended and toes pointed without faltering. She came out of her pose to sighs of envy and a small applause of admiration and praise, which she acknowledged with a cool smile and a nod of her head.

"Thank you, Miss Carter. That was beautifully done. We…" Rachel's praise was cut short as Damien touched her arm. "Um, Miss Carter, I wonder if you would mind performing the courting dance for us."

"Not at all," Natasha agreed even as her body groaned. Part of her wanted to go somewhere private and collapse, but she couldn't refuse—it was a wonderful sign this request was being made of her. She frantically ran through the dance in her mind, visualizing steps and combinations, praying she wouldn't forget any of them.

"I'll need a partner," she reminded.

"We haven't cast the male lead yet," Damien said as he stood and slowly walked toward her, "but I'm at your service, Miss Carter."

As he neared the stage, Natasha was quickly cognizant of the fact that Damien Johnson was even handsomer in person. His black hair was cropped close to his head, and a very light goatee accentuated his medium brown skin. His cheeks were chiseled and strong, and his full lips were smiling slightly. His body was magnificent—muscled, hard and completely masculine. He was dressed in black pants and black short-sleeved shirt stretched taut across his broad chest, which showed off his muscled arms. Lord in heaven, had she ever seen a more perfect man?

After an eternity, he finally reached her. Her tongue escaped to wet her suddenly dry lips. When his eyes darted to and fixated on her mouth, she let out her breath on an audible sigh. Trembling fingers smoothed an imaginary piece of hair away from her slightly flushed face, and she waited for him to speak because she couldn't; her tongue had suddenly become glued to the roof of her mouth.

"Shall we?"

Oh, Lord, his voice! It was deep, sexy and created very inappropriate visions in her mind of them pressed close, and not in preparation for dancing—at least not ballet dancing. Goodness, she had to get a grip on her runaway hormones where this man was concerned—a man she hoped would soon be her boss. His outstretched hand sent her into motion.

"Of course."

She forced the words through her constricted throat and took his hand—a hand that almost engulfed hers, a hand that she suddenly envisioned sliding caressingly down her trembling body. An electric shock went through them at that first contact. Their eyes darkened perceptibly as they silently stared at each other.

After interminable seconds, he nodded to the man sitting in the cave, and the music began. Before his disturbing eyes refocused on hers, she took a deep breath and released it slowly, silently reminding herself why she was here and to remain professionally cool and calm and to stop thinking like a woman when it came to Damien Johnson and behave like a dance partner instead.

The first strands were soft and sweet as they danced around each other, never coming too close, testing, teasing and tempting. She prayed she wouldn't miss any steps or embarrass herself by clinging to his hard, tempting body longer than their dance necessitated. Her heart was hammering loudly in her chest. Damien's focused eyes and expression were unreadable; she had no idea what he was thinking or feeling. They moved well together; she knew he hadn't danced professionally in years, but he was still very good. She came within an arm's length and then flitted away on the tips of her toes as the dance called for before twirling back into his waiting embrace.

What in reality took only several minutes to conclude seemed to stretch out endlessly. Finally, the music ended and they stopped close together. Her hands rested on his shoulders, and his were on her waist. Their bodies were touching lightly, and their lips were within centimeters of contact. Thunderous applause broke the spell that she was sure would have led to an inappropriate but very passionate kiss between them in a few more seconds.

"The best ballerina I've ever danced with." Damien's voice was for her ears alone as he reluctantly released her.

"You're too kind."

She told herself the breathlessness in her voice was a result of the dance, but she knew it had more to do with being held so close to Damien than anything else. She took a few necessary steps away from him, willing her heart to stop its frantic thudding.

"Just speaking the truth, Natasha," he said with a smile.

Her skin tingled at the sound of her name on his lips. It was as if no one else had ever spoken it correctly until him.

"Thank you."

"We'll let you know our decision in a few days." He abruptly turned and left her alone on the stage.

She stood there in a daze, not fully comprehending what had just happened before realizing she had been coolly dismissed. When no more requests were made of her, she turned and exited the stage, quickly making her way through her congratulatory peers and seeking the solitude of the changing room. Once there, she put cool hands to her burning cheeks and stared at her distressed expression in the full-length mirror.

So she had auditioned for and had danced with Damien Johnson. Her heart was still racing from the memory of being held close to his hard, masculine body and staring deeply into those expressive brown eyes of his. She felt completely raw, vulnerable and exhilarated in a way she never had before. She suddenly knew without a doubt her career and life were about to change in ways she had never imagined.

Two days and she still had not heard any news about her audition. Surely Damien Johnson had made a decision by now. A short while ago, she had ordered a pizza with the works, deciding to indulge herself in tons of calories and gooey cheese to soothe her nerves.

Sitting on her sofa, she absently surfed the web on her tablet before deliberately typing Damien's name into the search box. Her eyes widened at the plentiful results yielded, and she clicked on one link, followed by another and then another still. She came across multiple pictures of him with starlets and businesswomen, but none with dancers. Apparently he didn't go for ballerinas, which was reassuring; she had fought off more than her share of bosses who thought she would gladly trade sex for the lead, and she had no intention of going through that again. Whoa, she was getting a little ahead of herself; she hadn't even been offered the part—yet.

She clicked another link and began reading about an accident ten years ago in Atlanta—a bad one. That's when Damien had stopped dancing professionally. A woman had been driving, and he had been severely injured. As she scrolled down the page, she felt like a voyeur and glanced over her shoulder as if she would find Damien watching her disapprovingly. After investigating a few more links, her uneasiness about eavesdropping on his life intensified, so she quickly closed the page on her browser and sat her tablet aside.

She would hate to have her privacy invaded the way she was prying into Damien's past. Technology made it much too easy to snoop these days. She wasn't a nosy person; she was simply understandably curious about the man she prayed would soon offer her the chance of a lifetime. Of its own volition, her hand reached for the tablet again, but she determinedly pushed it away and instead picked up her iPod.

She scrolled through her playlists, bypassing her usual classical choices and choosing a rock and roll one instead before replacing the instrument in its dock. She plopped down into the middle of the tan-and-white sofa and stared out the glass balcony doors at the gorgeous Manhattan skyline—a scene which usually soothed her, but not tonight.

Taking a sip of Bordeaux, she reclined her head onto the back of the sofa but quickly snapped up again as the frenetic music she had chosen wafted through the air. Without hesitation, she moved her head to the beat and tapped her sock-covered feet in synch with the song.

She opened her mouth to sing along when the doorbell sounded. Picking up the remote, she turned down the volume, set down her wine, stood and walked over to greet the pizza man. No need to primp for him; she was sure he'd seen worse than her faded jeans, black T-shirt and hair in a ponytail. However, upon opening the door, cash in hand, the faint smile froze on her lips as her eyes encountered a smiling Damien.

"Mr. Johnson," she gasped.

"Hello, Natasha," he said.

"This is a surprise."

"A pleasant one, I hope."

"What are you doing here?" She couldn't process why the head of the ballet company would come to her door. No one got a job by having the boss come to the door.

"Is this any way to treat someone bringing good news?" He walked past her, inviting himself in.

"Good news?" Her eyes widened expectantly as she closed the door.

He glanced around the room that was a reflection of her personality—white carpet, pale tan-and-white furniture. She had hoped her design was elegant, yet cool.

He cocked his ear, listening. "I like your choice in music."

"Mr. Johnson…"

"Damien," he smilingly corrected. "This is a nice apartment for a struggling ballerina."

Her shoulders stiffened visibly. "Thanks."

He frowned at her frosty tone. "Did I say something wrong?"

"No." She shook her head, sighed and then decided to be blunt. "My father's a famous artist who owns a string of galleries, so technically I'm rich, but that doesn't mean I'm not completely dedicated to dancing."

"Of course it doesn't," he readily agreed. "Your financial status has no bearing on your talent—and you are talented."

His simple, honest words overwhelmed her until all she could manage was, "Thank you."

"You're welcome." He removed his jacket and folded it over one arm. "Now to the reason for my visit. I came to offer you the part."

Her heart pounded furiously in her chest. A brilliant smile lit up her face. She didn't know how it happened, but the next thing she knew, her body was pressed against his, her arms wound tightly around his neck while his rested lightly on her waist.

"Thank you!"

"I take it you're happy." He laughed at her exuberance.

Suddenly she realized the inappropriateness of her actions and self-consciously removed her arms from his neck and stepped back. Even though he was smiling at her, she was embarrassed. Lord, what he must think of her.

"I'm so sorry. I didn't mean…"

"No apologies necessary, Natasha." He smiled. "It's nice to know you really want the part."

"I do, very much."

"So—" his smile turned teasing "—I guess you're accepting my offer."

She stared at him, dumbfounded. Did he even have to ask that question?

"Of course I…"

Her voice trailed off as the doorbell sounded again. She excused herself to open it, but this time first looked through the peephole, revealing the pizza deliveryman.

"Hi." The man pulled a medium box from his red carrier. "That'll be $15.70."

"Hello." She briefly smiled, and held out the cash. Before the deliveryman could take the money, Damien had handed the man a twenty-dollar bill, took the pizza, thanked him then closed the door without collecting his change.

"You didn't have to buy my pizza."

"I did if I wanted to share it with you." He sat down on the sofa, placing the box, which he quickly opened, onto the coffee table.

"Damien…" She walked over and deliberately sat akimbo on the immaculate white carpet beside the glass table.

"Yes?" He smiled as he sniffed appreciatively at the loaded pizza. "How do you stay so small eating like this?"

"I'm blessed with a high metabolism, and I just felt like indulging myself tonight."

She fought to suppress a smile. He looked as happy as a little child on Christmas morning. His unexpected silliness was making her feel the same way—that and the knowledge that she was going to dance the lead in his ballet.

"Mmm." He picked off a mushroom and plopped it into his mouth, closing his eyes as if he were sampling a rare delicacy. "Lucky for me."

"Would you like some wine?" she asked with a laugh, unable to resist any longer.

"Love some." He tossed his jacket carelessly over the back of the sofa.

She stood to retrieve another glass and the wine bottle from the bar before pouring him a drink. Walking back to where he sat, she handed him the glass, resuming her seat on the floor in front of the sofa.

She picked up a slice of pizza and took a tiny bite, too excited to eat. Damien Johnson was in her home, and he was offering her the part of a lifetime; she was going to dance Juliet!

Suddenly, he took her hand, pulling her up onto the sofa beside him. She started to protest but decided against it.

"Tell me about yourself, Natasha."

"There's little to tell." She swallowed with difficulty. She couldn't breathe when he was this close to her.

"I doubt that." He took another drink of his wine. "How long have you been dancing?"

"Since I was five."

"You were brilliant in *Swan Lake*."

"Thanks." She sipped her wine. "I'm surprised you could pick me out of the ensemble."

"You danced the lead in a matinee performance," he reminded.

"How do you know that?"

"I was in the audience. Your performance was the reason you received an invitation to my tryouts."

"I only danced the lead in one performance when the lead was sick. It's lucky you picked that showing to attend."

He smiled. "Luck had nothing to do with it."

She frowned. "What do you mean?"

"I asked Ted Levy—" he dropped the name of her ex-director "—to let you dance that performance so I could see you onstage before an audience."

She nearly choked on her wine. "You what?"

He chuckled. "You heard me."

"I wish I had known I was auditioning."

"Why? You would have been too nervous had you known my intentions. My way was better."

She supposed he was right. Anyway, what did it matter now? Everything had worked out for the best.

"I tried out for the lead in that ballet and a lot of others."

"You didn't get it," he softly finished for her.

"No."

"And that bothers you?"

"No…yes." She paused and continued, "I don't want to sound conceited…"

"You don't." He touched her cheek tenderly. "Let's face it, Natasha. We both chose careers that are extremely hard for African-Americans to excel in."

"That's true," she agreed on a sigh. "But I never wanted to be anything else."

"You shouldn't be anything else. You're meant to dance."

She smiled at his genuine praise before admitting, "This is my chance, Damien."

"I know." He nodded his head.

He was so understanding—so genuine. She wasn't used to having anyone like him sympathize with her plight—

except her family, of course. In a few minutes, he had made her want to open up in ways no one else ever had. That realization unnerved her and prompted her to switch the focus of conversation onto him.

"How long since you stopped performing?"

His eyes clouded a little. "Ten years."

"Don't you miss it?"

"Some." He shrugged. "But I'm much more fueled by the creation and execution of the dance than actually performing."

"You're excellent at it," she praised. "All of your ballets received rave reviews. Everyone is expecting great things from this one, as well."

He winked at her. "And I don't intend to disappoint them."

"You won't."

"We won't." He squeezed her hand lightly.

From his reputation, she had expected him to be full of himself, but he was kind and utterly likeable. He didn't laugh at her, try to trample on her dreams, or expect anything from her as so many others had in the past. He seemed to genuinely believe in her talent—that she could dance the lead—and she wasn't going to disappoint him.

Unable to stop himself, he lightly fingered her cheek before moving down her jaw. He smiled when she gasped softly. His eyes lowered to inspect the pulse beating erratically at the base of her slender, graceful throat before his hungry gaze returned to her uneasy one.

She pulled back slightly, and his fingers fell away from her soft flesh. He leaned forward and picked up another slice of pizza. She took a drink of her wine and watched him silently for a few minutes. There was no denying the sexual tension between them was as thick as suffocating fog, but they were going to spend months in each other's presence and would have to come to an understanding of what their relationship would be.

"Damien, I don't want anyone to think that..." She paused, unsure of how to continue.

"What?"

She exhaled before continuing. "I don't want anyone to think that I didn't earn this part."

He stared at her silently for several seconds. She tried to discern what he was thinking. Had her unspoken worry been communicated to him? When understanding blossomed in his eyes and he smiled, she knew he appreciated her concern.

"People will think what they will, Natasha, but we both know the only reason you're going to dance Juliet is because you earned it, don't we?"

She returned his smile. "Yes, we do."

"Good." He stood and placed on his jacket. "Rehearsal starts tomorrow at 5:30 a.m. sharp."

"I'll be there," she assured while walking him to the door. "Thank you again for this opportunity, Damien."

"You don't owe me anything except a flawless performance." He touched her arm lightly before leaving.

Once alone, Natasha's smile turned into jubilant laughter. She pirouetted around the room before plopping happily down onto the sofa. She had done it; she was going to dance the part of Juliet! Snatching up the phone, she tried to decide who to call first—her parents, her sister or Erina, her coach. Tucking her legs underneath her, she dialed her parents' number. She couldn't wait until morning; tomorrow was going to be a fabulous day.

Chapter 2

At 4:05 a.m. Natasha made her way into the rehearsal hall. She was early purposefully; the extra time would allow her to warm up and be limber and ready to go when formal rehearsal started. She wanted to blow Damien Johnson away with her dancing and dedication—to show him she intended to give everything she had to Juliet.

She didn't see a soul, except the guard who let her into the building, as she made her way to an empty rehearsal room. She tugged off her leather jacket and sweatshirt, throwing them into a corner. Her shoes followed, being replaced by black ballet slippers. She twisted her hair back into a knot and decided to leave her white sweatpants on over her black leotards until she warmed up. She clipped her iPod onto her waist and pushed the earbuds into her ears, and without further ado she sat down on the cold hardwood floor to begin her workout.

Damien walked down the deserted hall on the way to

his office and frowned when he spied a light coming from a rehearsal room. He glanced at his watch; it was a little after four. Who besides himself was here at this hour? As he approached the doorway he stopped, and the frown on his mouth turned into a smile when he spotted Natasha sitting on the floor stretching. His prima ballerina was ready to go. Good. He would have been disappointed if she hadn't taken the initiative to come in early. She was ready to work hard, and he was more than willing to accommodate her.

He watched her for a few minutes as she went about her warm-up routine. She bent and contorted her body the way only a ballerina could before standing with her back toward him and walking over to the barre. Not wanting to interrupt, he took a step back until he was half-hidden by the door frame. She was so focused she didn't realize she was being observed. She effortlessly raised one leg even with the barre until it rested against it and then stretched both arms over her head, arching her back; the movement pressed her firm, round breasts forward, drawing his eyes to the perfect globes.

Lord, she was spectacular! She had the perfect ballerina form—tall and slender with graceful legs and arms, but she also possessed womanly curves. He remembered how good her soft, yielding body had felt when she had thrown herself into his arms last night when he had offered her the part; he had been pleased by the impulsiveness and pure joy she had exhibited. There was sweetness and vulnerability to Natasha that appealed to him. He knew he had made the right choice for Juliet.

He had read her resumé and talked to some of her former employers, who had stated part of the reason she had never achieved lead status with them was because she was simply too nice and unwilling to do what it took to win and keep the lead. Damien had read between the not-so-subtle lines, understanding that Natasha had been unwilling to buy the lead with her body, which he respected and admired.

He felt he understood her struggle for success; Lord knew he had undergone his own when he had started his company ten years ago. He had come up against one roadblock after another. But he had persevered, and with encouragement from Rachel and his family, he had kept plodding, dreaming and working until he now owned a world-famous company that a number of people said would never make it. Success really was the best revenge. He wanted that for Natasha. She was talented, hungry and dedicated; he was glad to offer her the chance she deserved to achieve her goals.

As he continued to watch her, he suddenly imagined those elegant limbs wrapped around him, holding him close while that perfect body trembled in passion against his—whoa, boy, where had that come from? She's your prima ballerina and your number one rule is to never get involved with dancers—especially those in your own company. Yes, she's beautiful. Yes, she made him feel something he hadn't in a long time, but they were here to work—nothing more, nothing less, and that's all he intended to do with her.

He turned from the door and nearly collided with a tall, thin woman with salt-and-pepper hair that was pulled back into a bun.

"Excuse me." He placed a steadying hand on her arm.

"It is quite all right," she responded in a slightly accented voice. "You are Damien Johnson, no?"

"Yes, I am, and you are?"

"I am Erina Deneuva, Natasha Carter's coach."

"Oh, I see." He nodded. "It's nice to meet you."

"You too." She shook his outstretched hand. "I hope you do not mind my presence. When Natasha called me last night with the wonderful news, she asked if I would come and work with her during this production."

"No, that's fine, as long as you understand I don't reimburse dancers for personal coaches."

"Of course." Erina smiled. "Natasha pays me as always, but even if she could not I would be here for her."

"That's an admirable thing to say."

"It is true. She is like a daughter to me."

"How long have you coached her?"

"For twenty-one years," she proudly answered. "We have been through a lot together."

"She's lucky to have someone so loyal."

"Thank you, Mr. Johnson."

"Call me Damien."

"Damien." Friendly hazel eyes met his. "Thank you for giving Natasha the chance she has long deserved."

"She earned it."

"She will not disappoint you."

"I know she won't."

"Can you tell me where I may find her?"

"She's in there—" he pointed behind him "—warming up."

"Excellent." Erina smiled. "If you will excuse me."

"Of course. It was nice to meet you, Erina."

"And you too, Damien." She smiled before entering the room where Natasha rehearsed.

After a few seconds he heard Natasha exclaim, "Erina, I did it!"

"Yes, you did. I am so proud of you."

"Thank you for coming on such short notice."

"Nonsense, child, where else would I be?"

"I still can't believe Damien Johnson came to my house to offer me the part."

"That is very unusual."

"Isn't it? I wonder why he did it."

"Who knows, but the main thing is that you got the part, no?"

"Yes." Her voice was bubbly with excitement. "I'm going to dance Juliet."

"Yes, you are. Now let us get down to work so that you will be brilliant, shall we?"

"I'm already warmed up."

"We will see." Erina's teasing voice elicited a laugh from Natasha. "Come, first position."

Outside in the hallway, Damien's smile turned to a slight frown. Rachel had also questioned his insistence on telling Natasha in person she was their choice for Juliet. He hadn't explained it to her satisfaction because he really hadn't understood it himself; telling Natasha in person had just been something he had wanted to do, and so he had. No big deal.

Shaking his head, he started down the hallway in the opposite direction. He had a million things to do before rehearsal started, and standing around contemplating his uncharacteristic behavior regarding Natasha wasn't one of them.

An hour and a half later, Natasha along with the other dancers stood in the main auditorium listening to Damien welcome them to the troupe.

"Good morning, everyone." Damien received echoing responses from the occupants of the room and continued. "First let me congratulate all of you on beating out stiff competition for your respective parts." He glanced at Natasha. "You are all here because you are the best and for no other reason."

He placed an arm around Rachel's shoulders, and hers went around his waist. "You all know Rachel Weston, casting director," Damien continued, "who is responsible in large part for your jobs."

"I'm highly susceptible to bribes—preferably chocolate." Rachel smiled, causing a round of laughter. "I'm glad to be working with all of you, and if this guy gives you any trouble, I'll do my best to get you out of it."

"I believe in hard work, and you may even come to think of me as an ogre." He paused, allowing his words to sink in.

"Truer words…" Rachel promised, causing another round of laughter, including Damien's.

"You keep me out of this." Damien affectionately scowled at her before continuing. "But I promise you once it's all over, the finished product will speak highly for itself." He glanced at his dancers, focusing on Natasha. "I'm going to drive you hard—probably harder than you've ever been driven before," he promised. "I apologize now for anything I might do to anger or offend anyone, because in two minutes when rehearsal starts, *I'm sorry* are two words you will never hear from me." He walked back center stage and his facial expression hardened slightly. "I'm a perfectionist, and I'll demand perfection from each of you. I'll receive it, or you won't be here," he sternly promised. "Any questions?" When none was forthcoming, he clapped his hands. "Okay, let's get to work."

"Let the fun begin." Rachel laughed as Damien joined her in front of the stage.

"Let's start with the ensembles." Damien began organizing groups. "The lead dancers should follow Ron and Carla, our assistant choreographers." He waved the group, including Natasha, away.

Natasha and fifteen other dancers entered a large white room whose walls were lined with brown wooden benches and ballet barres. She tightened the belt of her white wrap-around skirt, glancing up as a male dancer approached her.

"Hi." He extended his hand. "I'm Dennis, your partner."

"Hi." She shook his hand. "It's nice to meet you."

"You too." His appreciative eyes traveled over her face and body.

Natasha smiled tolerantly into his wolfish smiling eyes. It seemed she would have to put him in his place as she had numerous other partners in the past. He was tall, about six feet, with short black hair and dark brown skin. He definitely had a dancer's body. She couldn't help comparing him with Damien, who was a few inches taller and much more muscled and oh so more appealing.

"I can't wait to dance with you."

"We'll have plenty of opportunity for that."

"Hmm." He bobbed his eyebrows. "That suits me just fine."

"Dennis." She shook her head in remonstration. "We're here to work." She paused for emphasis before concluding, "And that's all I intend to do with you."

He sighed dramatically. "A guy can dream, can't he?"

She laughed. "Just make sure you can distinguish between fantasy and reality."

He grabbed her hand. "You're gonna give me an inferiority complex."

She chuckled. "I don't think there's much chance of that, Romeo."

He brought her hand to his lips. "You know, Juliet, I think I like you."

"I like you too, as a friend. Got it?"

"Got it," he echoed, kissing her cheek lingeringly. "But it's your loss."

"I think I'll survive." She playfully tapped his cheek, and he covered her hand with his before bringing it to his lips.

Damien chose that moment to stick his head in, and his eyes narrowed at the apparent intimate scene between Natasha and Dennis, though he made no comment. He couldn't blame the guy for being attracted to Natasha, but it seemed he would have to set Dennis straight about his strict no-fraternizing rule for his dancers; they were here to work, not engage in romance.

"Dennis, Natasha, let's try the courting dance."

Their heads turned in unison at his voice, and they moved to the center of the room. With Damien watching attentively, they performed the entire dance. "That was good, but I need it to be snappier and sexier." Damien walked over to them and took Natasha's hand. "Let me show you what I mean."

An effortless tug of his hand twirled her toward him and they began to dance. She vaguely registered the females were all swooning over him, and frankly she couldn't blame them. They didn't perform any strenuous moves, just teasing, testing, dancing close and moving away. They danced seductively, performing the same moves she had just done with Dennis; however, what had seemed tame with Dennis was positively scandalous with Damien. He touched her possessively as if it was his right, and their bodies were the perfect complements moving in complete sexy synchronization.

He suddenly pulled her to him tightly before almost throwing her away again. She pirouetted back en pointes on the top of her toes elegantly before darting away. She leaped toward him, and he caught her midair and then allowed her to slide ever so slowly down his hard muscled body, ensuring that she felt every wonderful inch of his unbending strength against her giving softness. Their eyes met and held hypnotically for several intense seconds that seemed like hours. The breath caught in her throat when his head levitated toward hers slightly as if he was going to kiss her.

He held her close for earth-shattering seconds before reluctantly releasing her. "See what I mean?"

"Yes, I think so." Dennis nodded in agreement.

"Yes," Natasha softly echoed.

She moved into Dennis's arms and noticed the immediate difference between the two men. Damien's powerful touch diminished Dennis's still-capable hands. She and Dennis mimicked the dance over and over again to perfect it. Damien fought down rising jealousy as they danced, as he had instructed and silently shouted at himself that this was about business; it wasn't personal. They were giving him and, more important, the dance what was required, and he had to remember that. Forcing himself to watch them objectively, he made them repeat the dance until he was satisfied with their performance.

"That's it." He smiled triumphantly after they had performed the full dance eight times in a row. "Take a break, you two."

Natasha and Dennis both heaved sighs of relief at his words. Dennis leaned against a nearby wall before sliding to the floor, and Natasha gratefully walked over and took a seat on a wooden bench to catch her breath for a few seconds. Damien was a perfectionist—good. So was she, and she would rehearse the dance one hundred times if that was required to perfect it. She stood and walked over to Dennis, taking his hands and pulling him to his feet to practice with her.

"Come on, Natasha, let me rest for a few minutes," Dennis complained.

"You can rest tonight at home." Natasha twirled into his arms. "Now, let's dance."

"All right." He sighed. "But if I step on your toes or pass out, you have only yourself to blame."

She laughed. "I've been warned."

Before Damien turned his attention to another pair of dancers, he glanced her way and smiled briefly in approval. She returned his smile before focusing on Dennis and their dance.

The day flew by and before she knew it, it was a little after 8:30 p.m., but she still wasn't ready to call it a night. She had never been so tired, nor felt so alive. She had thought Erina was a taskmaster, but she had nothing on Damien. He was a perfectionist, and she vowed she would be perfect for him.

Sounds of music echoed in the quiet as she rehearsed her first dance alone. She had tried to get Dennis to stick around, but he had moaned that a hot bath was calling to him. She smiled as she pirouetted around the room, improvising when she came to the part she would be dancing with Dennis.

"You need a partner."

She gasped and turned toward the door, where Damien leaned against the frame watching her.

"Damien, you startled me."

"Sorry." He walked over to her. "You still have energy left after rehearsals. That's admirable."

"This ballet is everything to me. I can rest after the performances are over."

"I like your attitude."

"I'm going to give you—the role of Juliet—everything I have, Damien. I won't fail you."

"I know." He smiled. "I sensed the drive in you. I'm glad you're not disappointing me."

"I won't, ever." Her eyes were deadly serious. "I promise."

That was a promise she intended to keep. This wonderful man was giving her the chance of a lifetime, and she would always be grateful to him for that. She wasn't used to having someone of Damien's caliber treat her with such respect and courtesy. She had other bosses in the past who had blatantly dangled the lead in her face in exchange for unlimited access to her body; vile offers that she had rejected. Damien had offered her the lead without even hinting that she repay him with anything other than hard work and brilliance. He possessed integrity—a trait she had started to believe no longer existed in the executive branches of the world of dance.

"I know you won't." He extended his hand. "Shall we?"

She hesitated for a second before taking his hand, allowing him to pull her close. She knew this was a mistake, but masochist that she was, she wanted to feel his arms around her. She had to stop thinking about him like this; he was her boss, and his offer to dance with her wasn't emotionally motivated—it was business.

"Where do we start?"

"At the beginning." He released her and walked over to select the appropriate music before returning.

When he placed both hands on her waist and maneuvered until her back was pressed against his muscled chest, every logical thought quickly fled from her mind, being replaced with inappropriate desire instead. The music began and they started dancing very close, yet bodies never intimately touching again; she always stayed just out of his reach.

They danced together for about fifteen minutes and he deliberately changed their steps so that they ended close together as they had begun, her back to his stomach—instead of an arm's length apart. He twirled her around to face him so that their lips were nearly touching and his arms were around her waist. Their rapidly beating hearts echoed the same intense rhythm—in part due to the dance, but in bigger part due to the obvious attraction that sprung to life when they touched that neither seemed capable of controlling.

After a few minutes, by silent mutual consent, they released each other and took a step backward away from temptation.

"I could use some water," Natasha spoke, simply to fill the uncomfortable silence.

"Me too." He walked to the door. "Let's see what's left in the break room."

She should refuse and leave, but she didn't. Instead she followed him out. Once in the deserted kitchen, she found a bottle of water and he opted for black coffee. They sat at a small table.

"So what do you think of the ballet?" He chose a nice, safe topic of conversation.

"It's wonderful." She smiled. "*Romeo and Juliet* has always been one of my favorites. I can't wait to perform."

"Nothing is more exciting than opening night," he agreed.

"Especially when you're dancing the lead."

"I'm glad you tried out for Juliet."

"So am I."

"Not to pat myself on the back, but my company is internationally known and many of my ballerinas are world famous. Why didn't you attend any of our open auditions?"

"I don't know." She shrugged. "I was busy working with other troupes."

She sensed he knew she was lying. She had wanted to prove she could make it in any troupe—not just an African-American one. That had been important to her, but now after years of frustration, she simply wanted to dance the lead.

"I'm glad the opportunity finally presented itself."

"So am I." She smiled at him, grateful for his obvious tact.

"You don't wear a lot of makeup, do you?"

"Excuse me?" She nearly choked on her water. "Do you think I need to?"

"Definitely not." He smiled and trailed a finger lightly down her cheek. His smile widened as he felt the shudder that passed through her at his actions. "You have the softest, smoothest skin."

"Thank you." Her voice was whisper soft.

His finger lingered maddeningly before eventually, reluctantly ending contact with her flesh. She felt bereft the second it did.

"Tell me what drives you, Natasha."

She shrugged, willing her heart to slow its frantic rhythm. "Work is my passion and my life."

He smiled in understanding. "A fellow workaholic."

"Definitely." She echoed his smile.

Suddenly for reasons he refused to examine, he wanted to know more about her, her life, her past. "Do you have a large family?"

She hesitated for a second before answering, "Average. My older brother, Nathan, is a lawyer. He lives in Washington. My younger sister, Nicole, dreams of being a famous fashion designer. She lives with our parents in Rochester. What about you?"

"Marcy, my sister, is a stockbroker like my dad," he said with some pride. "She lives here in the city, and our parents stay most weekends in the Hamptons. My mom's a partner in her law firm."

"Are you and your sister close?"

"Very."

"So are Nathan, Nicole and I." She sipped her water. "I can't wait to see them."

"You love them very much," he said with approval.

"Yes."

Her feeling toward her family pleased him because it echoed his and also because her genuine affection for them showed she could care about someone other than herself. She seemed steady and reliable and, thankfully, grounded— so unlike the psychopath he had the misfortune to get mixed up with ten years ago, Mia; her dysfunctional relationship with her family should have been his first clue that she wasn't playing with a full deck. But, Mia had been very good at pretending. When he remembered all the pain he had endured because of that maniac…

"Damien, are you all right?"

"Yes." He pulled himself out of his unpleasant memories. "I'm fine."

"Are you sure?" At his nod, her frown nearly disappeared. "Okay. Well, I think I'll head home. I'm beat."

"I don't doubt it. You put in a brutal day."

She sighed contentedly. "I loved every second of it."

"Good, because tomorrow will be just as long," he promised around a smile.

"I'll be prepared." She stood and he followed suit. "Good night."

"May I walk you home?" Why had he said that? It was the gentlemanly thing to do. That's why.

"No, thanks. I'll be fine."

"It's late. You shouldn't be walking the streets by yourself."

"I've lived in the city my entire life, and it isn't that late."

"All right." He shrugged as if it didn't matter. "See you in the morning."

"Good night."

Leaving her nearly untouched water on the table, she quickly left. She felt Damien's eyes boring into her back. She wanted to turn around but didn't. Instead she walked faster until she was no longer in his sight. She had to do something about her feelings for him, which were completely inappropriate and unexpected. She wasn't going to destroy this chance by lusting after her boss—no matter how handsome and kind he was, and the sooner her contrary body realized that fact, the better off she would be.

Chapter 3

Several nights later, Natasha walked into the Grand Ballroom of the Plaza Hotel on Dennis's arm. She wished her parents and sister were here, but her father's newest gallery was opening in Boston. They had wanted to postpone it, but Natasha had insisted they go since Erina would be with her and she would see them all in a few weeks.

She couldn't believe she was finally on the receiving end of a party introducing her as a prima ballerina. She glanced around the brightly lit ballroom, her eyes widening farther in awe. There had to be several hundred people in attendance. She had expected a much smaller event, but Damien had spared no expense—champagne fountains littered the room, exquisitely stacked buffet tables lined one side of the wall and elaborate ice sculptures were placed strategically throughout the ornate room that housed a multitude of sculpted stone pillars and sparkling crystal chandeliers.

Some of the hottest names in the ballet world were present, and they were here to see her. She felt like a princess and though the evening had just begun, she knew it was one she would never forget.

Her fingernails dug into Dennis's arm, causing him to wince slightly. "Hey, release the death grip."

"I'm sorry." She eased the pressure on his arm. "Can you believe all of this?"

"Relax," he whispered in her ear. "It's just a party. You've been to parties before."

"Not ones held to introduce me as a prima ballerina," she whispered back excitedly.

He glanced down into her overwhelmed face. "You're not going to faint on me, are you?"

"I hope not." Her grip tightened on his arm again.

"I know I have that effect on women." He smiled wryly. "But please don't."

She laughed as he intended, and her features relaxed somewhat. "I'll try to contain my pleasure at being your date."

"I'm surprised you asked me to escort you."

"Why?" She stared up at him. "We're friends, aren't we?"

"Of course, but I thought your boyfriend would bring you."

She shrugged. "I'm not seeing anyone currently."

"We could remedy that." His hand covered hers as it lay on his arm.

"Dennis, don't start that again." She shook her head in rebuke. "We work together, and it wouldn't be wise for us to date while we do."

His eyes twinkled. "Do you always do what's wise?"

"Always," she firmly informed him.

"What about when we're not working together?"

She smiled sweetly. "I hope that day never comes."

"I suppose I can't be mad at you for thinking that way."

"No, you can't. Now stop hitting on me and let's enjoy the party as friends, all right?"

"Deal." He kissed her cheek.

"Good evening, Natasha, Dennis."

Natasha glanced up to see a slightly frowning Damien standing in front of them. A tall slender woman was clinging to his arm as if she never intended to let go.

"Good evening, Damien." Natasha smiled at him. He looked wonderful dressed in a black tuxedo that accentuated his muscled physique.

"Hello, Damien, nice party." Dennis shook his hand.

"Thanks." Damien returned the other man's handshake. "This is Shelia Reynolds. Shelia, may I introduce Natasha Carter and Dennis Brown."

"Nice to meet you." Dennis and Natasha spoke simultaneously and then laughed.

"You too." Shelia coolly shook their hands.

Natasha noticed the woman's smile didn't quite reach her eyes and appeared phony—much as she did. Natasha was certain that her long straight hair was a weave and her red nails were false, as were a few of her body parts—particularly her buxom breasts that were straining against the revealing confines of the white gown she wore. She was pretty, if one leaned toward the dramatic.

"You look familiar." Dennis focused on Shelia. "Have we met before?"

At Dennis's innocent question, Shelia suddenly acted as if he had insulted her. Her lips thinned and she let out an audible disgruntled sigh.

"Well, I should. I'm the main character on *Today's World*," she indignantly named a top-rated reality show.

"Oh, well I don't watch the show, but good for you."

Natasha forced herself not to laugh at Dennis's perfectly aimed jab. As if sensing her struggle, he chuckled and placed an arm around her waist, a move she noticed seemed to intensify Damien's frown.

"Darling—" Shelia glanced at Dennis pointedly while pressing closer to Damien's side "—I could use a drink."

"In a minute." Damien extricated himself from his date and took Natasha's hand. "I need to introduce my prima ballerina to everyone."

Without another word, he pulled her away from their respective dates, both of whom were staring after them, flabbergasted at being deserted.

"Should we leave Dennis and Shelia like that?"

"They'll be fine," he dismissively replied. "I didn't know you were coming with Dennis."

"Is that a problem?"

"I hope not." He grabbed two glasses of champagne from a passing waiter and handed her one. "I don't allow romances between members of my troupe."

"Dennis and I aren't involved romantically."

"No?" Intense eyes bore into hers.

"No, we're just friends." At his raised eyebrow, she felt compelled to elaborate. "I didn't have a date for tonight, and he offered to escort me."

"I don't believe you couldn't get a date other than a fellow dancer."

"I didn't say I couldn't get a date. I said I didn't have one." She took a sip of her champagne. "I'm surprised you're not here with Rachel."

"She's here, but why would you think we'd come together?"

"You two just seem—close." She watched him furtively over the rim of her glass.

"We are, very."

"Oh, I see."

He arched an eyebrow. "What exactly do you see, Natasha?"

She glanced away from his penetrating gaze without answering, offering him the opportunity to appreciate her appearance unobtrusively. Her black floor-length gown was simple yet sexy with its sheer sleeves, high neckline and daringly low-cut back. The material clung to her curves in all the right places; she was, in a word, delectable. Never before had he been more aware of how beautiful she was than now seeing her all dressed up.

Diamond teardrop earrings hung from her ears, and her hair was pinned back into a flawless chignon. He had the ridiculous urge to release it and run his fingers through the soft strands. That's not all he wanted to do—her full, burgundy-colored lips begged to be kissed, which was an invitation he almost accepted.

"Come with me," he tersely ordered, taking her hand again and leading her onto the stage. They stopped in front of the orchestra, which at Damien's nod played an introduction, causing a hush to settle over the room.

"Good evening, ladies and gentlemen. I would like to thank all of you for coming tonight to help me celebrate and welcome a new prima ballerina to my troupe who will be dancing the lead in my next production, an original version of *Romeo and Juliet*. I look forward to great things from this exquisitely beautiful and supremely talented ballerina." He turned to Natasha and raised his glass. "May I present to you all, Natasha Carter."

Applause rang out. Natasha curtsied to the audience and clinked her glass with Damien's. They drank their champagne, eyes never leaving each other's. Her heart was thudding, not from the adulation being bestowed on her, but rather from the way he was staring at her. Before she could contemplate exactly what she had seen in his eyes, he took her hand and helped her down from the platform and took her around to introduce her to some of the elite guests.

Natasha was blown away by the guest list; everyone who was anyone in the ballet world was present and seemed enthralled with Damien. The guests treated her to the kind of admiration she had always dreamed of receiving, but had begun to think she would never achieve.

"Thank you for this, Damien," she spoke when they were relatively alone again. "This is fabulous."

"It's no more than you deserve."

His easily uttered, sincere words touched her heart. She felt close to crying from the utter happiness she felt at the moment—due in large part to Damien. She suddenly wanted to grab him, pull him close and never let him go. For the life of her, she didn't know how she resisted.

"Shouldn't you get back to Shelia?"

"Trying to get rid of me?"

"No, of course not." She glanced across the room, where Shelia stood with her arms crossed, glaring at them. "It's just that she doesn't seem very happy."

Damien chuckled. "Don't worry about Shelia. I'm not." To prove his point, he took her glass, deposited it along with his own onto a nearby table and pulled her into the center of the room, where various couples were dancing.

"What are you doing?" she whispered in shock.

He pulled her close. "I'm dancing with my prima ballerina."

"I don't think this is wise."

"Why not?"

She glanced around the room; a lot of eyes were glued to them. "People will talk."

He shrugged. "It's expected that I dance with you. Besides, it's not as if we're naked, rolling around on satin sheets."

His words conjured up forbidden images, which she fought mightily to dispel. Why did he have to say that? Now she would have that not-unpleasant idea in her head for the remainder of the night.

"You're the one who said you don't allow dating between troupe members."

"We're not dating." His hand pressed against her bare back. "We're dancing."

"I know, but…" Her voice trailed off as his fingers lightly strummed against her spine.

"Besides, I'm the boss, I make the rules." He smiled at her roguishly. "But I don't have to follow them."

"Oh." She wasn't quite sure how she should take that statement. Was he teasing her, or was he hinting at something forbidden?

He twirled her around the floor, pressing her body tighter against his unyielding one. She fought to maintain her composure. They had danced before, but not like this. Maybe it was because parts of their bare flesh touched or because here and now they were a man and a woman instead of two dancers rehearsing. She didn't know, but whatever the reason, this dance was systematically destroying her second by wonderful second. She contradictorily found herself praying for it to both end and go on and on. She was in trouble, and she had no idea of how she had fallen into peril or how to extricate herself from it.

"Damien, I'm tired. I'd like to sit down."

"You spend fourteen hours a day every day dancing strenuously, and a few minutes of slow dancing with me have worn you out?"

Put like that it sounded ridiculous, but she couldn't help it. If she didn't get out of his arms right now, she was going to do something foolish and embarrass both of them.

"People are staring," she lamely informed.

He glanced pointedly around the room. No one was paying them any undue attention. When he gazed back into her distressed eyes, he smiled slightly. "No they're not."

"Please." She pulled against his hand. "You don't want to be the subject of gossip, and neither do I."

"One thing you'll learn about me, Natasha, is that I don't live my life by other people's rules," he promised before releasing her suddenly. "Thanks for the dance."

Before she could respond, he had walked away, leaving her in the middle of the dance floor. She tried not to feel abandoned, because he had done as she had asked. She slowly walked over to pick up another glass of champagne and silently cursed herself for missing Damien's company.

As Damien slowly walked back to his date, a smile played about his lips. He had enjoyed his brief time with Natasha and would have prolonged it, had he not been fighting a strong urge to kiss her tempting lips. How had someone so pure survived in the cutthroat world of dance for years as she had? She made him feel alive in ways he hadn't in years; she was so fresh and, frankly, naïve, and he was completely intrigued by her.

"So you finally remembered me?" Shelia said when he stopped by her side.

"How could I forget you?" Damien's suddenly bored eyes drifted over his date's angry countenance.

"I don't appreciate being abandoned for Bambi," Shelia made her displeasure known.

His eyes narrowed. "First of all, this party is for *Natasha,* not you. Secondly, you don't now nor will you ever own me. I do what I want when I want. Thirdly, if you're not having a good time, no one's forcing you to stay."

"Damien." She grabbed his arm as he turned to walk away. "I'm sorry. It's just that I was all alone."

"I'm sure you weren't traumatized for the few minutes I attended to the guest of honor."

"Don't be too sure." She placed a hand on his chest and pressed close. "Now that you've done your duty, why don't we get out of here and go back to my place?"

"Maybe later. I still have a lot of mingling to do." He disentangled his arm from her fingers. "Are you coming, or do you want me to have a car take you home?"

His demeanor made it crystal clear he was fine with whichever option she chose. Shelia was a readily available date when he needed one. She wasn't the type of woman he could ever be serious about, which he supposed was her appeal. She had used some of his contacts in entertainment to further her career. In fact, he had gotten her the audition for her current job, so she couldn't complain about their casual on-call arrangement.

"I'm coming with you." She walked over and linked her arm through his.

"Suit yourself," he said and shrugged.

As they walked toward the buffet tables, his eyes automatically scanned the immense crowd for Natasha—the woman he really wanted at his side for the remainder of the party.

"Congratulations, Natasha."

"Thanks, Rachel." Natasha scanned the crowd. "Have you seen Dennis?"

"A few minutes ago. I think he was heading toward the buffet."

"I should go find him."

"He'll keep for a minute." Rachel placed a halting hand on her arm. "You and Damien looked good together on the dance floor."

"He was just being polite."

"I doubt that." Rachel laughed. "There's no law against you two dancing."

"I know, but his date didn't seem too happy about it."

"Shelia?" Rachel shrugged dismissively. "She's overly melodramatic. I think it stems from her acting career."

"You don't sound like you like her."

"Oh, she's all right."

"Why didn't you come with Damien tonight?"

Rachel smiled. "Damien and I are good friends. We don't date each other."

"Have you ever?" Natasha didn't know why she was feeling so bold, but she couldn't seem to stop the questions from exiting her mouth.

"No." At Natasha's obvious interest, Rachel decided to elaborate. "We met about eleven years ago when I was choreographing a ballet he was dancing in. We hit it off and have been friends ever since."

"Oh." Natasha smiled brightly. "That's nice."

"That information pleases you."

"No, not at all." Natasha quickly denied. "I just…"

"Are you interested in Damien?"

"Damien has a no-dating policy for his troupe," Natasha sidestepped her question. "I had to assure him tonight Dennis and I are just friends."

"Really?" Rachel raised an eyebrow.

"His concern was professional, of course," Natasha quickly added.

"Of course." Rachel didn't look convinced. "But you still didn't answer my question—are you interested in Damien romantically?"

Natasha chose her words carefully. "Rachel, I like Damien. He's been kind to me. But I've worked too long and too hard for this opportunity to jeopardize it."

"All that's true, but…"

"There you are." Dennis touched Natasha's arm. "I was beginning to feel ditched."

Natasha could have kissed him for interrupting Rachel's inquisition. She was quickly running out of ways to deny that she did have inappropriate feelings for Damien.

"I'm sorry." Natasha took his hand. "I promise to be a perfect, attentive date for the remainder of the evening."

"I'm going to hold you to that one." He pulled her toward the dance floor. "Excuse us, Rachel?"

"Of course. Have fun."

Rachel watched the two leave with mixed emotions. Natasha appeared to be honest and focused on her career, but she also was interested in Damien. She couldn't blame her, but she had no intention of standing idly by again the way she had ten years ago while Damien got hurt. She intended to keep an eye on Natasha, just in case she wasn't what she appeared to be.

As Natasha danced with Dennis, she found herself wishing she was being held in Damien's strong arms again. Of their own volition, her seeking eyes found Damien, who stood several feet away with Shelia close by his side. Natasha suppressed a shudder as Damien's intense gaze held hers for several moments before Dennis innocently led her away. She steeled herself not to seek out Damien's gaze again, but she felt his burning eyes on her several times through the remainder of the evening, though he never physically sought her out, much to her dismay.

It was the best night of her life; it was also the most revealing, because seeing Damien with another woman made her realize that despite her good intentions, despite the inappropriateness of it, despite the innumerable reasons why she shouldn't, she was developing feelings for her boss— feelings that she silently vowed to keep in check, somehow.

Chapter 4

The next morning at 4:00 a.m. Natasha walked into work, stifling a yawn behind her hand. After a night of merriment, she had somehow dragged herself out of bed at her usual time. She performed her morning workout and, humming music from the ballet, entered the rehearsal hall promptly at 5:30 sharp. Once rehearsal began, however, she quickly realized this was going to be a long, difficult day.

"No, no, no!" Damien shot out of his chair and walked toward the stage and quickly up the steps. "Natasha, what are you doing?"

"I'm dancing."

"Is that what you called it?" An eyebrow rose mockingly as he reached her side.

She bristled at his insult, even though it was justified. She wasn't at her best today; her mind had been wandering to the wonderful party last night.

"I'm…" His angry look cut her words short.

"This is the passionate part of the dance, and you're not doing it right. You're not crisp enough! You're being stilted, careless and cold!" He screamed the words at her.

"I'm sorry." His criticism stung all the more because it was warranted.

"I don't want your apology." He folded his arms across his broad chest as he glared at her. "I have to have passion from you. *Passion!* Do you know what that is?"

She bit her lower lip hard to stem the tears that wanted so desperately to escape from her eyes. She would not cry in front of him. She was a prima ballerina and she could take stinging criticism—especially when it was justified. He wanted passion, and she would show him passion.

"May I try it again?"

"You'd better." He scowled as he walked off the stage.

She took a deep breath and released it, glanced at Erina, who gave her thumbs up for encouragement, and then began to dance. She must have done better, because this time Damien didn't interrupt her, though when she finished he was still frowning.

"Again," was all he said.

She performed the dance for the third, fourth and a fifth time before he allowed her to stop. She was breathing hard from exhaustion, but she was prepared to perform again until Damien was satisfied.

"That was adequate." Some of the bite left his voice. "But it still needs work."

She took heart in his words. At least he wasn't screaming at her anymore, and in her book that was major progress.

"I'll give it special attention."

"Yes, you will." He nodded curtly. "Dennis, try it with her."

"Yes, sir." Dennis took her hand and whispered in her ear, "You'll get it."

Natasha offered him a slight smile. "I will."

"All right, you two, let's go," Damien ordered impatiently.

"Yes, sir," they echoed in unison and began to dance.

The other dancers breathed a collective sigh of relief, glad Damien's anger wasn't directed at them. This was the first time they had seen him lose his temper, and it wasn't a pretty sight. Once lunch came, everyone was overjoyed for the break.

Natasha stood in front of her coach in a small rehearsal hall occupied by only the two of them. She chewed on her lower lip as Erina sternly lectured her.

"You are a prima ballerina now, Natasha," Erina reminded. "More is expected of you than just being good. You must be great."

"I know."

"You were sloppy in rehearsal." Erina touched her shoulder. "And you know it."

"I guess I was distracted," she admitted.

Erina frowned. "By what?"

"I was thinking about my party last night."

Erina allowed her expression to soften. "It was a spectacular event, no?"

"It was better than I ever dreamed." Natasha beamed. "Damien went overboard, didn't he?"

"Mr. Johnson appreciates your talent, and you deserved every heap of praise you received."

Natasha hugged her coach close and kissed her cheek. "Oh, I love you, Erina. You know that, right?"

"Of course I know that." Erina returned her hug for a few seconds. "Now, we must put that type of emotion into your dance. Come now, let us practice, and when you return to stage, you will, how do you say, knock Mr. Johnson's socks off."

"Yes," Natasha smilingly agreed.

"Let's begin. First position. Now stretch," Erina instructed. "Good. Bend more, more. Good."

Erina ordered one difficult exercise after the other without hesitation, challenging Natasha's strength and resolve. Natasha performed each maneuver without complaint; she was intent on being perfect when rehearsal continued, and hard work was what it took to be perfect.

About twenty minutes later, neither of them saw Damien, who had stopped in the doorway to observe his prima ballerina. He watched Natasha's limber body arching and bending effortlessly. The lovely female curves strained against the thin leotard, leaving nothing to the imagination. He remembered the feel of that soft body pressed close to his last night and insanely craved a taste of her sumptuous lips; would they be as sweet as he imagined?

He felt an answering response in his loins as he unobtrusively watched her. He had put her through the ringers this morning, and she hadn't complained—not once; instead she had worked harder, trying to deliver the performance he demanded. During the past week, his belief that she was a gifted, dedicated ballerina had been confirmed. She wasn't a diva or a troublemaker; all she wanted was to dance. He hadn't found any faults with her, personally or professionally.

Why did she have to be so damned beautiful inside and out, making him want her so much? And God help him, he did want her, but he knew he couldn't have her. Purposeful denial was a distasteful state he didn't intend to become accustomed to; he wasn't used to denying himself anything—however, he knew that was exactly what he must do when it came to his craving for Natasha.

"Jeté, jeté, now fouetté." Erina briskly called out different moves, which Natasha performed without stopping. "Good." Erina beamed as she completed each maneuver. "Now, let us end up at the barre."

Natasha quickly complied. After such a vigorous workout, she needed some relaxing time at the barre to stretch out her limbs. She placed a slender leg over the wood barre and then rose with her hands stretching toward the ceiling. Her back was arched. She held the position for at least a minute before relaxing and lowering her arms.

Natasha opened her eyes, and he watched her pupils dilate in surprise at finding him watching her with a look of barely restrained hunger. His eyes darkened intensely before he turned and walked away before she could say anything and more important, before he acted upon the strong impulse to pull her into his arms and fuse their mouths together for interminable minutes.

"Was someone there, Natasha?" Erina frowned at her pupil's shocked expression.

"No, no one," Natasha lied, dabbing her face with a towel.

How long had Damien stood there watching her? Had she really seen desire in his eyes directed at her, or had she imagined that? One thing was certain: she felt as if she had been stripped naked and ravaged on the spot—much to her chagrin, she wished she had been.

After rehearsing with Erina for an hour, Natasha continued working out in one of the training rooms with her friend, Simone. She gracefully rose from a plié before lowering to perform another. She was determined that when rehearsal resumed, she would dance flawlessly.

"Natasha, sit down and enjoy your lunch," Simone said reproachfully.

"I'm done." She raised her leg even with the barre and began stretching.

"You haven't finished your salad."

"You know that Damien likes to test our stamina in the afternoon." She lowered her leg from the bar and slowly extended it behind her. "Besides, after this morning, I want to be perfect."

"This morning was tense." Simone took a sip of her water.

"That's an understatement." Natasha rolled her eyes.

"Well, you handled it perfectly, and by the end of rehearsal Damien seemed happy with your efforts."

She sighed. "I hope so." The last thing she wanted was to face his wrath again.

"Why were you so off-kilter?"

"I don't know." She shrugged. "Maybe all the excitement last night."

"It was a fabulous party, wasn't it?"

"Yes." Natasha smiled dreamily at the memory. "I didn't expect anything so extravagant."

"Why not? You're a prima ballerina now."

"I know, but more than anything all I want is my chance in the spotlight dancing the lead on opening night."

"In a few months you'll get your chance."

"And I can't wait." Natasha's smile brightened.

"It will be here before you know it," Simone predicted.

"I hope so." Natasha's smile was replaced with determination. "But for now, I'd better try and make it through rehearsal without angering the boss again."

Simone laughed. "I think that's an excellent plan."

"Natasha." Dennis walked into the room, interrupting their conversation. "Want to go over our prelude dance?"

"Definitely." Natasha turned to face her partner. "I can use all the practice I can get after this morning."

"Well, come then, let's get it on." He bobbed his eyebrows dramatically.

"You're such an idiot." Natasha laughed and took his hand, throwing over her shoulder, "Excuse me, Simone."

"Sure." Simone stood. "I need to do some stretching myself."

Dennis placed a hand on the small of her back to lead her to the other side of the room, where he twirled her around before pulling her close. She laughed into his smiling face and pushed out of his arms, but he laughingly pulled her back.

"It was a great shindig last night."

"Yes, it was."

"I had a blast with you." He began to sway with her in his arms.

"I had fun with you too."

"We could have more fun if you'd just say the word."

"Dennis, I like you very much—as a friend."

"Why not more?" He bent her backward and then pulled her back up to face him.

"Two reasons." She pressed out of his arms. "First, I don't want to destroy our friendship by trying to be more. And second, but more important, Damien doesn't like his dancers to date, and I'm not going to do anything to jeopardize my position here."

He sighed and kissed her hand. "Two very good reasons that I can't argue with—especially the last one."

"Good, now can we get to work?"

He sighed in resignation. "That's what we're here for."

"Yes, it is," she agreed, tapping his cheek playfully before pirouetting away from him.

Dennis was a dear and she liked him, but they would never be anything but friends. He didn't make her heart flutter and cause the breath to freeze in her throat, refusing to exit her lungs properly, the way Damien did. At the forbidden thought about Damien, she again silently lectured herself—Damien was her boss; she was his prima ballerina, and they would never be anything else—period. At least, she tried to add a period behind that declarative statement; however, despite her best efforts, it didn't seem to fit where Damien was concerned.

Damien entered his office and found Rachel sitting behind his desk.

"What are you doing rifling through my desk?"

"Oh, hi." Rachel playfully extended her palms in his direction. "You're not going to turn your foul temper on me, are you?"

He chuckled. "That depends on why you're here."

"I'm looking for the music for the second act. Do you have it?"

"Move." He held out his hand and helped her to her feet before sitting down and opening the center drawer of his desk, retrieving a CD and sheet music. "Here."

"Thanks." She perched on the edge of his desk.

He reclined in his chair. "What else can I do for you?"

"Nothing."

"Come on, Rachel," he said and sighed. "Out with it."

She smiled before asking, "Did you see Natasha?"

"She was rehearsing with Erina, but I didn't speak to her. Why?"

"I thought maybe you would seek her out and apologize."

An eyebrow rose arrogantly. "Apologize for what?"

"You were a little hard on her this morning."

"Hard?" Damien laughed. "Compared to what I'm really capable of, I was downright pleasant."

"Yes, you can be a devil," Rachel agreed on a laugh. "Did she complain to you?"

Even as he asked the question, he knew the answer. Natasha wasn't one to complain.

"No, of course not," Rachel admitted. "I was just surprised to see you tear into her."

"Why?" He sat forward. "I have a ballet to put on and precious little time to get my dancers ready."

"True, but you're attracted to Natasha. That was obvious last night."

"Last night I was playing the host. Natasha's my prima ballerina, and that's all."

"Is that why you personally went to offer her the job and why you take every opportunity to dance with her?"

He sighed. "I went to her house because I know what it's like to need someone to give you a chance. I feel a sense of empathy with her. Is that a crime?"

"No, of course it isn't."

"And she's not the first ballerina I've ever danced with."

"No, but she is the first ballerina you seek out opportunities to dance with."

"I do no such thing."

"Say what?" Rachel chuckled. "Please, Damien. You can fool other people and even yourself, but not me. I've known you too long. Your entire demeanor changes when you're in the same room with Natasha."

Yes, you're right. I can sense Natasha's presence without even seeing her. There is an attraction between us, but regardless of how difficult it is to resist, I have no intention of acting on it—no matter how much I hate denying myself anything.

Aloud he responded, "You're seeing things that aren't there."

"I just don't want history to repeat itself." All humor quickly dissipated. "I should have spoken up when you started dating that witch, Mia. I promised myself I'd never make that mistake again."

"Hey." He reached across and took her hand. "That wasn't your fault."

"I knew she was trouble, and I should have said something when I learned you were dating her. But I didn't know how you would take it, and I didn't want to risk losing your friendship if you thought I was just telling tales out of school."

"What matters is that when I asked, you told me the truth about her and stopped me from marrying her when she faked her pregnancy. I'll always be grateful for that." He stood and kissed her cheek. "I'm a lot older, wiser and a much better judge of character now." He felt compelled to add, "Believe me, Natasha is nothing like Mia."

His words piqued her curiosity. "How do you know that?"

"For one thing, as you know, part of our hiring process included a thorough investigation of Natasha's work history—interviews with colleagues and employers. Nothing alarming was found. Secondly, I've talked personally to her several times—gotten to know her a little—and I'm encouraged by what I've learned and witnessed in her so far."

"And from a conversation or two, you think you know what motivates her?"

"My gut tells me she's sincere and independent. She doesn't want anyone to give her anything—she wants to earn it."

"All admirable traits."

"They are." He smiled slightly before continuing, "She's also trusting, strong and persistent—not needy and manipulative the way Mia was. Natasha's not like anyone I've ever known."

Rachel watched him closely. "You sound taken with her."

"I simply admire her tenacity in holding on to her dreams—not giving up when she got kicked in the teeth again and again. She's a fighter."

"Sounds like she's made quite an impression on you."

"She's a nice lady whose quest for success I can identify with."

"I just don't want you to be hurt again."

"Believe me—" his eyes hardened "—I won't be. Mia's deceit taught me well."

"I'm glad to hear that." Rachel placed a hand on his shoulder. "Despite all of my questions, I agree that Natasha seems as different from Mia as night is from day."

He shook his head in exasperation. "Then why have you spent the last five minutes grilling me about her?"

"Because we both know the dangers an in-house romance can create."

"We do," he sighed and said in agreement. "Which is why I've never engaged in one since Mia, and I have no intention of starting one now."

"Okay. I'm done butting my nose in your business—for today at least."

"Good." Damien walked around his desk. "You don't have to worry. My interest in Natasha is purely professional. Now, let's get back to rehearsal."

When Damien and Rachel entered the rehearsal hall, all of the main dancers were onstage, including Natasha and Dennis, who were laughing. Damien frowned as Dennis reached out, took Natasha's hand and twirled her around playfully before pulling her close and bending her backward with his body close to hers before slowly returning her to an upright position. He twirled her away from him and then she pirouetted back until she was close by his side again, his arm draped around her waist, her hands resting on his shoulders. Natasha laughed at something he whispered in her ear before pushing out of his arms, though she continued to hold his hand.

Damien fought down an insane rush of something that felt like jealousy as he watched the familiar exchange between them. They were just friends. There was no law against that. He had made his feelings about anything more between them known last night, and he knew Natasha understood his concerns and wouldn't cross the line with Dennis. But he still didn't like the way Dennis looked at her.

"Why are you staring at me, Rachel?" Damien questioned without removing his eyes from the laughing couple onstage.

"Why do you think?"

He sighed. "I hate it when people answer a question with a question."

Rachel laughed. "You know what I hate?"

He tore his eyes away from Natasha to frown at her. "I'm sure you're going to tell me."

She touched his cheek. "People who *evade* questions."

"Rachel." He removed her hand from his face. "Please don't start that again. Nothing untoward is going on."

"If you say so."

Without responding, his eyes returned to the stage, where Natasha was watching them. She quickly turned away and continued dancing.

"All right, let's get started everyone," Damien ordered, focusing everyone's attention on him.

"Natasha, Dennis, let's try your dance from Act 1, Scene 3."

"Yes, sir."

"Hopefully it will be up to par this time."

"It will, sir," Natasha promised with a slight smile.

"We'll see." He nodded to Rachel, who started the music, and then he settled onto his stool beside her for the remainder of rehearsal.

Chapter 5

Natasha entered a deli near the rehearsal hall with Dennis, Simone and four other dancers after rehearsals around 8:45 p.m. Natasha would have rather gone home, but she had been talked into coming by Simone. They pushed two tables together, and she sat down with Dennis on one side of her and Simone on the other.

"Look, Damien and Rachel are here." All eyes turned in the direction Simone pointed.

"Great," Dennis groaned, and Natasha echoed his sentiments.

Simone studied everyone's face. "Should we go over and say something?"

"No, I don't think that's a good idea," Natasha quickly dissuaded.

"Neither do I," Dennis agreed. "After the day he put us through, I really don't want to talk to the guy until I have to at rehearsal tomorrow."

"Well, I can't blame you for that." Simone laughed. "He certainly lived up to his reputation for being a perfectionist."

"That's much too nice a way to put it." Dennis scowled and stretched his arm along the back of Natasha's chair.

Everyone laughed at his disdainful tones, except Natasha. She was too uncomfortable—wondering whether or not Damien thought she was on a date with Dennis. She sincerely hoped he didn't think she was trying to date her partner on the sly. After furtively glancing over at his table and connecting with his frowning face, she wasn't so sure about that. She knew she should have followed her instincts and gone home.

Damien's brooding eyes fixated on her. Even from the distance separating them, she sensed his displeasure at the scene he was witnessing. She groaned inwardly before lowering her gaze and concentrating on the conversation of her friends, trying to forget Damien was here, somehow.

Rachel glanced up from Damien's tablet as the waitress placed her drink on the table. Giving the woman a smiling nod, she spied several members of the troupe sitting down at a table across the room.

"Looks like we're not the only ones who decided to eat out tonight." Rachel's statement necessitated Damien refocusing on her.

His jaw was set in a hard line. He picked up his drink and downed half the contents.

"Looks like it."

Rachel frowned at his demeanor. "What's wrong?"

"I told Natasha to cool it with Dennis."

Rachel eyed him curiously. "They just seem like friends to me. Besides, they're with a group—not much of a romantic date."

"I realize that," he snapped at her.

"What *is* the matter with you?"

"I don't like being disobeyed."

Natasha looked as uncomfortable as he was angry. Good. He sadistically hoped she didn't enjoy a second of her dinner, because he wasn't—not with her sitting so close and cozy with Dennis.

"No one's disobeying you," Rachel contradicted. "They're just having dinner."

"I don't want anything to interfere with my ballet, and as you reminded me earlier, an in-troupe romance could wreak havoc."

"I agree." Rachel studied him closely. "But are you sure you're referring to Natasha and Dennis?"

"Who else would I be talking about?" At her pressing look, he continued, "Back off, Rachel."

Rachel held up her hands in surrender. "If you say nothing is going on between you and Natasha, I believe you." *As much as I believe it will be one hundred degrees tomorrow.*

"Finally," he said with a scowl.

Snatching up his menu, he pretended to study the contents, all the while trying to forget that the woman he found himself constantly thinking about was just a few feet away—so near and yet so unobtainable.

The next day at rehearsal Natasha thought she was dancing perfectly, but she soon found out that there was going to be no pleasing Damien. He was intent upon finding fault with everything she did.

"Dammit, Natasha, will you follow my instructions!"

The hair on the back of her neck stood on end as he yelled at her for what seemed like the hundredth time in the past three hours, and she was sick of it! She had been distracted yesterday, but today she was focused like a laser beam.

"I thought I was."

"Well, you thought wrong," he said and scowled. "I've explained what I want five times. How many more will you require before it sinks in?"

Before she could answer, he stalked onstage, glaring at her all the while, and danced his instructions for her. His eyes blazed angrily once he had finished the steps he wanted her to mimic.

"Now, do you think you can do that?"

"Yes." She perfectly performed the combination he had just illustrated. "How was that?" Her eyes challenged as she stopped in front of him.

"It'll do for now." He nearly barked the words as he angrily turned to exit the stage.

"Lord, give me strength to…" Her words were spoken under her breath and were cut short when he turned to glare at her.

No one was safe from Damien's wrath, as the company soon found out. The dancing wasn't right, the music wasn't right, the atmosphere wasn't right, the lighting wasn't right. Nothing was right.

He knew he was behaving like an ass, but he couldn't seem to help himself. He was on edge, and the beautiful, desirable reason for his irritation was staring at him dumbfounded from the stage. He had spent the better part of last night going over reasons why Natasha was off-limits to him, but none of the logical facts had succeeded in dampening his damned attraction to her.

She and Dennis began to rehearse their dance again while he watched intently. He was just looking for something to find displeasure with, however minute it might be, and he found it.

"Natasha, you're being stilted and unbending." Damien's stinging criticism halted their dancing. He walked to the stage and pushed Dennis aside, taking his place. "Try it with me."

They danced for a few seconds and she kept her body rigid, refusing to relax against his no matter how good it felt to be close to him, despite his foul demeanor. She refused to look at him, keeping her eyes fixated on his shoulder.

"Dammit, woman." He stopped abruptly. "It's like dancing with a mannequin!"

She indignantly placed her hands on her slender hips, readying herself for a royal battle of wills. She could take criticism as well as anyone, when it was justified. She didn't understand Damien's displeasure with her; she was dancing from her heart and soul today and hadn't made a single mistake.

"I don't know what you want," she verbalized her frustration.

"Obviously," he dryly responded. "If you are not ready to perform to my standards, you should have stayed at home!"

Her hands curled at her sides into fists, and somehow she bit back the angry words that sprang to her lips. She was not going to argue with him in front of the entire company; it was unprofessional. She silently counted to ten when he turned to say something to Rachel, who quickly sprung onto the stage and started talking to him in hushed, urgent whispers. Natasha appreciated the other woman's efforts; at least she wasn't the only one who knew Damien was behaving unreasonably.

Damien held up a silencing hand and turned from Rachel's angry countenance. Then he motioned for Dennis to resume as her partner. He curtly nodded his head to the pianist to start playing and watched the two dancers, ready to pounce on any perceived mistake.

Natasha inhaled and exhaled deeply. Dennis pulled her to and fro like a yo-yo, but she refused to complain and simply flowed with the music and reacted to Damien's frequently spoken directions. An hour and a half later, when they finished their sixth attempt, her body ached, but it was worth it as she received the first words of praise from Damien's frowning mouth that she had heard all day.

"That was beautifully done, Natasha. Why did I have to fight you so hard to get it out of you?"

He turned and walked offstage before she could respond. Shaking her head in confusion, she stared at his retreating back. As a ballerina, she thought she was supposed to be the temperamental one. This was certainly shaping up to be an eventful day; she silently prayed for a nice boring one tomorrow.

At the end of the day, Damien passed by Natasha's dressing room, by accident, he insisted upon telling himself. The truth was that they had shared a tumultuous day together due entirely to his bad mood, and he wanted to clear the air.

He stuck his head through the open door. "May I come in?"

"Of course." Cool eyes met his briefly.

He sighed audibly. Obviously, she was still angry about his behavior today. He supposed he couldn't blame her; he had been impossible to deal with, as Rachel had pointedly informed him several times.

Natasha was dressed in street clothes—denim leggings and a red figure-hugging long-sleeve blouse—and her hair was pulled back in a ponytail. The outfit accentuated her feminine curves, and, as always, she looked beautiful—and desirable.

"I know I was a bear today."

Natasha pointedly glanced up before lowering her gaze to pull on a black leather ankle boot, but remained deafeningly silent.

He sighed before sitting down opposite her. "Natasha, look at me."

After a slight hesitation, she did as he asked. "Why were you so angry today?"

"It was just a bad day for me. Haven't you ever had one of those?"

She wanted to ask what had made it so bad, but thought better of it; he was trying to be civil, and frankly she had enough of his foul temper to last her for a good while.

"Too numerous to count." She gave him a brief smile before bending down to place on her other boot. "I suppose we all do once in a while."

"We're all under a lot of pressure to get this ballet ready in time, and I guess I was just feeling it today."

"That's understandable."

"Then you forgive me?"

Her eyes widened in surprised shock. He was her boss; what did he care what she thought? Why was her forgiveness necessary to him?

"Natasha, truce?" He prompted when she remained silent, "What are you thinking?"

"Hmm?" She jumped slightly. "Nothing." She reached out and shook his offered hand. "Truce."

He didn't release her hand immediately. His grip was firm and caressing. When his thumb slid across the back of her hand, a jolt of crippling awareness shot through to her core.

"Do you like ice skating?"

She blinked. "What?"

"Ice skating." He smiled. "Do you like it?"

"Yes, I love it."

"Good." He pulled her upright. "Come to Rockefeller Center with me then."

Her eyes widened. "Now?"

"Why not?"

"I don't…"

"Do you have other plans?"

"No."

"You really can't skate, you're so tired you can't make the walk, you're allergic to ice." He smilingly rattled off excuses.

Despite her apprehension, she laughed. "No, none of those things."

He watched the indecision in her eyes. "Come on, consider it more practice."

She laughed. "I suppose I could."

"Then let's go." He pulled her toward the open door, stopping long enough for her to grab her jacket.

She should refuse. She knew she should refuse, but for the first time all day, they were finally behaving civilly toward each other, and glancing into his smiling, hopeful eyes, she didn't have the heart to disappoint him—or herself.

"Okay," she agreed.

She allowed herself to be led laughingly from her dressing room. They exited the building and walked down Fifth Avenue until they reached Forty-Ninth Street and entered Rockefeller Center. They rented some skates, laced them up and made their way onto the half-occupied ice.

They effortlessly skated to the center of the ice, and he took her hand and skated off. Natasha quickly learned Damien was a great skater—perhaps even better than she was and that was saying something, since Erina had introduced her to skating when she was five.

They pair skated and he lowered her into a death spiral that rivaled any professional skater's before pulling her upright and into his arms, where they performed an impromptu ice-dancing routine. Before long, other skaters were watching their display with claps and cheers, and when they skidded to a halt, they received a round of applause. Damien soon had everyone organized into line skating, cajoling the young and old into participating regardless of their skating prowess or lack thereof. Finally, at Natasha's urging, they formed one enormous human chain with everyone holding hands. They skated faster and faster around the rink until they all collapsed into a laughing, exhausted heap on the ice.

They spent about forty-five minutes interacting with the other skaters, and it was the most fun Natasha had ever spent on the ice. She marveled at how easily Damien brought out the fun part in her that had been dormant for far too long.

"That was so much fun." She laughed as they leaned against the railing to catch their breath.

"I think everyone enjoyed it."

"I've skated here hundreds of times, but I've never mingled with the other skaters before," she confessed.

"Why not?"

She shrugged. "I was practicing."

"You have to learn to enjoy yourself more."

"You may be right."

"I'm always right."

She laughed. "I'll remember that."

"Are you too tired for more?"

"No way." She took his hand and followed him back onto the ice.

They skated hand in hand, and he twirled her around expertly into a pair spin at such a high rate of speed she was dizzy when they stopped. She leaned into his hard body for balance. Her hands were pressed against his chest, and his rested on her waist. They stared deeply into each other's eyes—each knowing they should move away, yet unable to do so. The smiles on their lips died.

Natasha's heart skipped several beats as she waited for Damien's next move. Never releasing her, he moved his face closer to hers. One of his hands left her waist to cup her jaw, drawing her nearer. His thumb caressed her smooth cheek. They gravitated together centimeter by centimeter until their lips touched lightly in butterfly kisses at first, but then the dam quickly broke and his mouth demanded and hers surrendered.

They quickly forgot everyone around them and lost themselves in each other. His lips were warm, firm and insistent. Had she ever been kissed so thoroughly or devastatingly? Absolutely not. She leaned into his hard body for support against the sensual onslaught laying siege to her carefully constructed control. His fingers pulled the elastic band from her hair, allowing his fingers to entwine in the soft strands.

Suddenly, she didn't care who might see them; the only thing that mattered was that Damien keep kissing her for as long as she lived. Her fingers dug into his solid shoulders as she hung on for dear life while their mouths sensually acquainted themselves. Their tongues met halfway, and when they touched, white-hot lava erupted from deep within them.

God, what was he doing? Even as he silently asked the question, he was unable to stop. He had longed for this since she had breezed into his life a few weeks ago, and when her fingers anchored to the back of his head, pressing his mouth tighter against hers, he knew she had wanted the same. His arms reached around her waist and hers encircled his neck as they lost themselves to sensation.

Who knows how long they might have kissed had not good-natured catcalls, whistles and claps from bystanders echoed loudly in their ears. Reluctantly, they pulled apart and laughed at the skaters watching them with amusement.

"We have an audience." Natasha glanced around self-consciously before returning her eyes to Damien's.

He smiled wolfishly. "Then let's give them something to really look at."

The fingers entangled in her hair guided her sweet lips back to his as he devoured the delicacy of her luscious mouth. She wound her arms tighter around his neck and hung on for dear life.

When she entered the deserted rehearsal hall early the next morning as was her routine, Damien let her into the building, which was unusual. Had he been waiting for her? Her heart fluttered nervously at the sight of him. This was the moment she had dreaded all night—not knowing how to react to him after their scandalous kisses last night.

"Good morning, Natasha. I'd like to see you in my office."

Without waiting for her response, he walked away down the hall and she followed. A frown turned down the corners of her mouth. This wasn't exactly the type of greeting she had anticipated from him. Admittedly, after their kisses she had left him at the ice rink, begging a headache, and walked herself home, but surely he must have understood how confused and upset she had been by them crossing the forbidden line between them.

Once they reached his office, he closed the door for privacy despite the fact that no one else from the troupe was present yet. He leaned against his desk, crossed his arms over his broad chest and stared at her silently for a few uncomfortable seconds.

"I thought we should clear the air before everyone gets here."

"All right." She waited for him to speak.

He came straight to the point. "Last night's kiss was a mistake."

She balked at his dismissive reference to last night. She supposed for a man of his reputation, that's all it had been, but for her... What had it meant to her? She wasn't sure, but it definitely hadn't felt casual or ordinary.

"It was?"

"Yes." He smiled tolerantly. "We just got carried away in the moment."

"I suppose we did."

"And we're not going to let it interfere with our work. Right?"

"Definitely not." She forced a rigid smile.

He continued in emotionless tones, "It won't happen again."

"No."

"Why don't you go ahead and get in your morning work-out."

Being dismissed, she slowly walked away and silently chided herself. Of course the kiss had meant nothing to him; it had meant nothing to her either. She wanted that to be the truth—she assured herself it was the truth; however, deep down inside, she knew it was a lie.

After morning practice, she didn't see him at all. Instead, Rachel took over rehearsals, which was highly unusual. Instead of being glad to have some breathing room to sort out her feelings, she was instead disturbed by his absence. By early evening break time, she had worked up the nerve to seek him out and try to dispel the unease that had developed between them since last night. She found him in his office, his head bent over his laptop screen, notepad beside him and a pencil perched between his white teeth.

"Damien, can I talk to you?"

He glanced up briefly and removed the pencil from his mouth. "What is it?"

She sighed inwardly at his cool tones. Why was she here? He had made his position clear this morning, and he was right. So why was she here?

"Well?" He sat back and waited for her response.

"I missed you at rehearsal."

"Did you?" He smiled without humor. "Why?"

"Well…" She smoothed her palm down the chocolate skirt covering her matching leotards. "Because you're usually there."

"I have a lot on my plate, and Rachel's perfectly capable of taking over for me from time to time."

"Of course she is." His coldness caused her to act like an idiot, not knowing what to say.

"What do you want, Natasha?"

He quickly grew weary of being in the same space as her and being unable to touch her, which was why he had Rachel take over rehearsals. He reminded himself the distance between them was necessary. He needed to get a rein on his ever-growing desire for her, which he knew he couldn't act upon.

Last night had been a mistake—he had asked her skating to prove to himself that once he spent some time alone with her, he wouldn't want to spend any more; however, that had backfired on him badly. He had a great time with her last night, and it only made him want to spend more time alone with her, getting to know her better, which was impossible. And of course he had done the unthinkable and kissed her—Lord, he could still feel her soft, responsive lips pressed close to his. The memory had been torturing him all day long.

"I have a question about the changes Rachel made to the courting dance."

It was a lame reason and she knew it, but she didn't know what else to say. His demeanor made it impossible for her to really say what was on her mind.

"Shouldn't you speak to her about that?"

Without waiting for her response, he returned his full attention to the computer screen and began typing some information on the keyboard. She continued to stand before him as he worked.

"I suppose I should."

He impatiently glanced up again. "I think she's in rehearsal hall two." He bent his head over his notebook, and as she hovered, he looked up again. "Is there anything else?"

"No." She backed away. "Thanks."

He made no comment as he went back to his work. She turned and slowly left. When she had gone, he raised his head and pushed away from his desk to go after her, but stopped himself. This was for the best—no matter how rotten it felt, it was for the best. Sighing, he returned his attention to his notebook and concentrated on work instead of his gnawing need for Natasha.

For a nanosecond, he thought about calling up Shelia for a date; she was always up to helping him blow off steam. The problem with her, though, was that she created far more tension in him with her ever-present drama than she ever relieved, and one thing he had enough of in his life currently was tension. Besides, he didn't want to spend time with Shelia or anyone else—he wanted to be with the woman whose company he thoroughly enjoyed—Natasha.

Damn! How had this happened? Last night with her had been more fun than he had experienced in a long time. She filled a purposeful emptiness in him and made him want to trust again—something he wasn't sure he was capable of anymore. Trusting was dangerous; it led to vulnerability, and that in turn led to possible heartache, which was something he had experienced enough of in this lifetime. Still, denying his attraction to Natasha was becoming nearly impossible, and he honestly didn't know how much longer he could do it.

As Natasha walked away from Damien's office, she was more confused than ever. Despite Damien's assertion that their kiss had been a mistake, she knew he had felt the desire spring to life between them, and she sensed he was trying to deal with their troubling attraction as professionally as he could; hence his newfound aloofness toward her. He was doing the right thing; they had crossed a forbidden line last night—one that must never be breached again. She knew that. She understood that. However, she hated every single, wretched second of having to pretend she felt nothing for him, when the truth was she felt far too much.

Chapter 6

It was a little over a month before Thanksgiving and Damien was hosting the lead cast, a total of sixteen dancers, at a lodge in Saratoga Springs for an intensive week of work while his assistants stayed in Manhattan to spruce up the background dancers.

Natasha slowly maneuvered her Jeep through snow-covered roads. It had been snowing when she left Manhattan, but the farther north she had gone, the worse the storm had become. Erina had stayed in New York; having student appointments that she couldn't break, she was unable to be away from the city for a full week. Though Natasha longed to have her lifelong mentor with her, she understood and had assured her she would work hard.

Natasha had plenty of company for the trip though, as she was part of a caravan making its way to the retreat. She glanced at Simone, who sat in the passenger seat, and

Dennis along with Simone's partner, who were bundled in the back.

"It's really coming down." Simone peered out the frosted window. "Isn't it?"

"In buckets." Natasha nodded, keeping her eyes glued to the road.

"Want me to drive?" Dennis offered, sitting forward.

"No thanks. I think we're almost there."

"I hope so." Dennis stretched his arms as much as possible. "My body is getting stiff."

"Don't worry." Natasha smiled at him through the rearview mirror. "Once we get there, I'm sure Damien will work all stiffness out of you."

"Truly." Dennis laughed before sitting back and closing his eyes.

After about thirty more minutes of tense driving, she pulled up outside the main building of the rustic yet modernized lodge and let out an audible sigh of relief. It took her a few moments even to release the steering wheel. She didn't think she would ever drive again! She was no sooner out of the car and into the thankfully now-diminishing snow, than she felt Dennis take her hand and laughingly pull her into the welcoming shelter of the lodge.

"What about our bags?" Natasha glanced toward the trunk, where Simone stood.

"I'll come back for them once we're checked in," Dennis promised.

Damien and Rachel met them in the lobby. Damien's eyes narrowed when Dennis escorted a laughing Natasha into the lodge. When she saw him, she released Dennis's hand and removed her hat, never completely meeting his eyes, he noticed in annoyance. Damien's lips curled into a frown. Obviously Natasha and Dennis had driven down together—a fact that irritated him.

"Welcome, everyone." Damien gathered them in a semi-circle. "We've already checked you in. Take two hours to unpack and explore the lodge, and meet me in the rehearsal hall at—" he glanced at his watch "—twelve-fifteen. You'll find directions at the front desk."

Everyone murmured agreement and took keys from either Damien or Rachel. Natasha's and Damien's fingers touched slightly when she took her key; she quickly retrieved her hand, pretending not to notice the slight lifting of his eyebrow at her action. She wanted to say something but didn't know what; therefore, she offered a small smile before walking upstairs with Simone to find her room.

About twenty minutes later, showered and changed into black jeans, knee-high black leather boots, white sweater and a black leather parka with fur trim, Natasha made her way outside into the crisp air. Her hair was pulled back in a ponytail, and since her jacket contained a hood, she didn't wear a hat.

She should have been situated in front of a fire or, better still, warming up before rehearsal; however, she had the urge to unwind and get away from everyone before rehearsal began. She had just planned to take a quick walk around the grounds, but as she wandered through the four or five inches of fluffy snow that covered the feet and ankles of her boots, she found herself getting farther and farther from the main lodge until she came upon a tall white building. She warily approached the brown door and opened it, delighted to find herself in a barn. She walked inside and approached several stalls occupied with horses. She slowly approached a black horse with a white diamond shape on its forehead and nearly jumped out of her skin when Damien stood from adjusting a stirrup.

"Damien." A hand flew to her throat. "I didn't know anyone was in here."

"Neither did I." He pulled his gloves from his pockets and placed them on.

"I'll go and leave you alone." She turned to leave.

"You don't have to."

His words halted her, and she turned to face him again. "Are you sure?"

He sighed. "Natasha, we're both adults. We can be alone together."

She wasn't so sure about that. When she was alone with him, the most inappropriate thoughts ran rampant through her mind; it had been three weeks since their kisses, and Damien seemed unaffected by memories that still plagued her. Perhaps she was being silly; there was no reason they couldn't be friendly.

"I suppose we can," she finally agreed.

He smiled, as if aware of her turbulent thoughts. "How's your room?"

"It's wonderful." She smiled genuinely. "I didn't expect to have a private one."

"The main leads have private rooms." He assured that her accommodations were nothing out of the ordinary. "Everyone else has a bunkmate."

"Oh." She cautiously approached a stall to examine a horse more closely. "Aren't you pretty?"

"Go ahead and rub him," he prodded. "He won't bite."

She looked doubtful. "Are you sure?"

"You're not afraid of horses, are you?"

"I don't think so." She warily extended her hand and touched the horse's nose and laughed when it bobbed its head in response. "I've never been this close before."

"You're kidding."

"No. I've always wanted to learn to ride, but I never got around to taking lessons."

"Well, ma'am, you've come to the right place." He bowed formally. "Allow me to instruct you."

"Seriously?"

"Sure." He led his horse out of its stall. "We have plenty of time before rehearsal starts for a quick lesson."

"On second thought, Damien, I don't think that's..."

"Natasha, we're only going to ride—" he paused before wickedly concluding "—horses."

She gulped at his double entendre. His smile widened, informing her he was well aware of her discomfort. She intended to refuse his offer, but she didn't for two reasons: she wanted to learn to ride and, more important, she wanted to spend some time alone with him no matter how ill-advised that was.

"All right," she acquiesced. "If you're sure you don't mind."

"I'm sure."

He quickly saddled a brown mare, which thankfully looked a lot tamer than the one he was planning to ride, and helped her into the saddle. Touching her waist to position her properly, he showed her how to mount the horse. With his help, she foisted herself up into the saddle and was proud she stayed put instead of toppling off the other side.

Damien quickly mounted his horse. "How does it feel?"

"Strange, but good." She laughed in wonder. "It's like I'm ten feet tall."

He smiled. "You are, thanks to your friend."

"What do I do now?"

"Take the reins, one in both hands. When you want to go right, you pull on the right one, and vice versa for going left. If you pull back on both, you stop. It's really very easy once you get the hang of it."

"If you say so." She looked skeptical.

"Trust me." He smiled. "We won't worry about galloping today, since this is your first lesson. We're just going to go at a nice, slow trot."

"That sounds perfect."

"Nudge him a little with your knees and pull on the left rein to get him going."

She did, and her eyes widened when the magnificent beast began a slow walk toward the open barn door.

"Don't be afraid. I'm right behind you."

"Okay." She nervously glanced over her shoulder for a second.

Once they were out of the barn, Damien steered his horse to walk beside hers, and she felt much better being able to see him. He was so close, their legs brushed against each other's. Their long stare acknowledged they felt the electric jolt that shot through them at the contact, but neither made any verbal comment about it.

It felt wonderful sitting on the back of such a strong yet gentle animal. Exhilaration like she had never experienced before assailed her from her high perch; it was a feeling she quickly became addicted to.

"We'll keep to the path," Damien instructed. After a few minutes, he asked, "How you doing?"

"Fine." She finally allowed her face to relax into a tentative smile. "In fact, this is great."

"It's a one-of-a-kind feeling, isn't it?" Happiness spread through him at her obvious enjoyment. "You're doing great."

"Thanks." She laughed. "I can't believe I'm doing this."

"Why haven't you ridden before?"

She shrugged. "I just never seemed to have the time."

He wagged a finger at her. "You have to make time to enjoy life, Natasha."

"I guess I should." She continued without thinking, "I always have fun when I go out with you."

He stopped his horse, and his smile echoed her sentiments. What was it about her that beckoned to him? Maybe it was the joy she exhibited in the smallest things, or her genuine innocence, or perhaps it was her willingness to go above and beyond to be the best ballerina she could. More important, maybe it was the astounding fact that she, without even trying, made him feel so much—happiness, contentment and, of course, dizzying passion.

They rode in silence for a while until the lodge wasn't visible. All that stood in front of them were snow-covered trees and a pure blanket of white, untouched snow covering the ground.

"What's your favorite food?" Natasha queried out of the blue.

"Lasagna," he automatically answered. "And yours?"

"Momma's pot roast." She sighed appreciatively. "You've not lived until you taste that."

"I'll look forward to it."

His innocent words thrilled her. She silently hoped he would be around to experience that, and much more, with her. She knew she was in trouble, but a foray into forbidden territory had beckoned to her since meeting Damien, and it was one invitation she was having the hardest time declining.

"Favorite movie?" she asked to quiet her forbidden thoughts.

"Star Wars." His response was quick and definitive. "That was the first movie I saw that started an epic journey that lives on until this day." He stroked his horse's mane. "What about you?"

"I think it would be *Psycho*—the original one with Anthony Perkins."

"You're a horror aficionado?"

"Absolutely." She laughed. "I surprised you, didn't I? You thought I would say I don't have time to watch movies."

Her mock-serious tone had him laughing too—something he did easily around her. By mutual consent, they dismounted and walked the horses through snow for a short while before tying them to a white fence. They continued to walk slowly side by side.

She glanced up at him. "Best thing to do in the snow?"

He bent down and picked up a handful of snow and began forming a ball. She held up her hands in warning and began backing away from him.

"Damien, don't you dare throw that at me!"

"You asked." He smiled devilishly and let the ball fly. It swooshed over her head as she ducked.

"Now you've done it." She formed her own ball, belting him on his left shoulder.

Soon they were embroiled in a full-fledged snowball fight, hiding behind an occasional tree to escape being pelted. Suddenly, Damien effortlessly picked her up and unceremoniously dumped her into a mound of snow before covering her body with his. They were laughing like children, which quickly turned into groans when their lips inevitably touched as Damien thoroughly ate the clinging snow from her face and mouth, and when she shivered, switched their positions so that he was lying with his back pressed into the snow and she was lying on top of him.

Their mouths met again—this time in a kiss that should have instantaneously melted the ice in which they lay. He kissed her slowly, languidly, warming her cool lips with his, causing heat to coil within her stomach and slowly spread through her entire body, as she was pulled close against his solid frame.

His hands moved to her buttocks as his lips hardened on hers—everything suddenly forgotten, except need. Giving in to an overpowering desire to feel her naked skin, Damien hastily removed his gloves and tossed them onto the ground, exposing his hands to the cold air.

His now-bare fingers insinuated themselves underneath her jacket, slowly moving up her sides to the sides of her breasts, kneading her flesh through her lacy bra until she was groaning against his lips. Then his hands moved up her back to her neck until his fingers reached her hair, releasing it from its tidy ponytail until her soft, straight tresses tumbled down to caress his hands. He slowly ran his fingers through the silky strands, pulling her mouth closer to his as his lips slanted over hers. His tongue aggressively massaged hers before sucking it into his mouth, and dizzying desire began to flame within each of them to the point of incineration.

They kissed hungrily for a few stolen moments before he sat up and then stood with her still in his arms, mouths still clinging tight. Her mouth opened wider beneath the aggression of his as he continued to plunder and devastate. She wrapped her legs around his waist as he carried her effortlessly back to their horses. Her fingers dug into his muscled shoulders, bracing against the emotional onslaught his skillful hands created.

When he slowly released her clinging mouth, she ran kisses over his face. "I love your face. You're so handsome."

"Same goes." He bit into her earlobe.

"You think I'm handsome?" She indignantly smirked, cupping his face between her palms.

"You're the most beautiful woman I've ever seen," he seriously replied. "It should be a crime for a woman to be so beautiful," he whispered before capturing her lips again.

His words caused her heart to swell in happiness until she thought it would burst free from her chest. It was then and there she knew she was fighting a losing battle trying to ignore her feelings for this man.

When their lips reluctantly parted again, they were both breathing hard. There was so much they could have said, but both thought it wiser to leave the words unspoken—for now.

"We'd better get back," Damien suggested.

"Yes," she softly agreed, lowering her feet to the ground.

They returned to their horses hand in hand and, once sitting in their respective saddles, made their way back to the stables in relative silence. Each was lost in deep, contemplative thoughts.

When they reached the barn about twenty minutes later, Damien helped her dismount. His hands remained on her waist, and serious eyes bore into hers. She knew what he was going to say before he uttered the words.

"About our kiss, Natasha."

"We just got carried away." She smiled slightly. "Right?"

He chuckled at her choice of words. "We seem to do a lot of that, don't we?"

"Yes," she softly agreed. "What are we going to do about it?"

"Nothing." He released her and took a step back. "We both know why we can't get involved."

"Agreed."

That wasn't how she felt. There was so much more she could have said—wanted to say—but didn't. She sensed he wanted to say more too but, like her, held back.

"Why don't you go ahead inside, and I'll take care of the horses."

If she stood there one second longer staring at him with those longing, unsatisfied eyes, he was going to pull her to the ground, make thorough love to her and let the consequences be damned.

"All right." She hesitantly took a step away and turned. "Thanks for my lesson."

He smiled slightly. "You're welcome."

They parted ways, and the next time they saw each other was at rehearsal, where they both acted normally as if nothing had happened between them. Yet every time she looked at him, she knew he was transported back to memories of the kisses they had shared earlier in the snow—just as she was.

Rehearsal lasted until seven forty-five that night, and after dinner everyone retired to their respective room to rest up for the 5 a.m. call in the morning. Natasha had been in her room for two hours trying to sleep. However, she was too restless; her mind insisted on replaying her scorching kisses with Damien earlier.

Finally, at eleven, she decided to go down to the rehearsal hall and work on the scene that had given her trouble today so that she would be perfect in the morning. Maybe once that was done, she would be so exhausted that her mind would stop thinking inappropriate thoughts about her boss and sleep would finally claim her.

Damien strolled into the rehearsal hall around 11:15 p.m. and frowned when he heard soft music from the ballet playing. Maybe Rachel was working late. Instead, he found Natasha dressed in navy sweats onstage dancing her heart out. A smile lit up the corners of his mouth as he silently admitted the reason for his insomnia—he had wanted to see her, but had thought better of going to her room at this late hour because he had known that course of action would have led to the forbidden pleasure he was trying so hard to resist.

"Don't you ever rest?"

Natasha jumped at Damien's voice and then nervously laughed. "When I sleep. What are you doing here?"

"I needed some music." He explained his presence as he ascended the stage. "I've worked with lots of ballerinas, but I've never met one more dedicated than you."

"Thank you."

He stopped a short distance from her. "It's a crime you've never had the opportunity to dance the lead until now."

"It's been hard," she admitted. "But I believe things happen when they're supposed to. I have my chance now, and I intend to make the most of it."

"You'll be brilliant." He added with a wink, "Once I whip you into shape."

She laughed and curtsied gracefully. "I am the clay and you are the sculptor."

His eyes darkened at her assertion. "Really?" He walked closer and took her hand. "I like the sound of that."

Her eyes widened. "What are you doing?"

"Molding my clay." He pulled her close and they began to slow dance. He added appreciatively, "My supple, soft clay."

Her heart stopped beating for a few seconds before resuming madly. This wasn't a good idea. She should say good-night and leave, but instead her free hand rose to his shoulder and his rested possessively on her lower back.

They stared at each other longingly before starting to dance—not ballet, but close and seductive, barely moving, staring deeply into each other's eyes. The fingers of his free hand snaked under her top to caress her warm flesh and found, to his delight, she wasn't wearing a bra. He watched her eyes widen and then cloud, as her breathing hitched in her throat.

He moved until he stood behind her, one arm around her waist, hand resting possessively on her flat stomach. His other hand held hers close to her side. He pressed his front to her back tightly so that she had no doubt about his desire for her. They were so close, a sheet of paper couldn't fit between them.

The palm against her stomach rubbed down and then back up before stilling again, and he smiled slightly when he felt her tremble in response. Purposefully the hand holding hers moved until her palm was resting against his stubbly cheek, and his fingers entwined with hers, keeping her hand in place against his face.

He held her close and his warm breath caressed her, starting a sweet ache in her stomach that radiated outwards to all parts of her now-tingling body. She silently prayed that he would have mercy and release her, and at the same time she prayed he would hold her forever.

His hand snaked up her ribcage slowly to rest just beneath her left, aching breast. Her breath caught in her throat, and she bit her lower lip to hold in the moan that wanted so desperately to escape. He lowered his head and rubbed his slightly scratchy cheek against her soft one, and her eyelids drooped as white-hot desire shot through her center.

She soon realized this was a purposefully choreographed, maddening seduction, and Damien performed it flawlessly and demanded nothing less than the same from her. He never let her get very far from his hard body while he made love to her on the stage. Almost instantaneously, blind animal lust took over. She allowed herself to throw caution to the wind and respond to him the way they both wanted.

She loved being held by him—loved the way their bodies felt when pressed intimately tight. They fit so well together, as if they had been made for the sole purpose of joining; he was the perfect half that completed her. His hand slid to her inner thigh, turning her around and hooking her leg over his hip, pulling her so close against his hardness that she audibly groaned. He smiled slightly before bending her backward and rubbing his lower body sensually against hers. When he pulled her upright again, his eyes were dark with a need she was certain hers echoed.

How long they silently seduced each other she didn't

know. It seemed as endless as it was effortless. They ended close, facing each other. One hand was fastened to the back of her head, and the other was pressed against her lower back. Her arms were wound around his neck. Their lips were a hair's breadth apart; she could feel their breath intermingling as one. She was trembling, aching, and only he could soothe the sweet pain he had created deep within her.

Did he move first, or did she? She didn't know, but suddenly their lips touched, and it was enough to ignite a wildfire that instantly blazed out of control. They kissed hotly, feverishly before Damien slowed things down, taking his time tasting every flavor her honeyed lips and mouth had to offer. She returned the kiss, fervor for fervor, and soon was lost yet found.

Merciless desire coiled in them, intensifying agonizingly. They pressed closer as their mouths once again engaged in frenzied exploration, silently vowing to leave no crevice unexplored—completely focused on thoroughly feeding the ravenous hunger that had been growing within them since their first dance.

"I can't take more of this torture," Damien groaned against her ear after prying his lips from hers.

"Neither can I." She sighed the words.

"These last weeks of behaving antiseptically around you have been agonizing."

"They have been for me," she agreed. "The distance between us didn't seem to affect you, though."

"I was pretending it didn't." His mouth settled in the soft skin of her neck before he lifted his head to stare at her longingly. "I thought that was best for both of us."

"Now you don't?" Her hands ran down his broad back. "Until you kissed me earlier today, I thought you didn't want me."

"Oh, I want you." He rubbed his mouth against hers

fleetingly. "I've tried not to want you, but I might as well have tried to stop breathing—that's how impossible it was."

"I feel the same way."

They stared at each other while trying to find the resolve to walk away from temptation. Neither of them was capable of exercising it this time.

"Come to my room with me before we go insane." He arrived at a long-overdue decision. "It's what we both need."

Chapter 7

His heartfelt plea was all the encouragement she needed. Yes, she knew the reasons they shouldn't let this happen, but nothing that felt this right could possibly be wrong.

"I do need you," she finally admitted.

"Then come with me." He held out his hand to her.

She hesitated for a second before placing her hand in his. They walked then nearly ran up the flight of stairs, quickly moving through the thankfully deserted halls until they reached his huge suite, containing a kitchen, living area and bedroom. Vaguely she made note it was decorated with heavy mahogany furniture and dark colors: chocolate brown, black and white.

Natasha turned into Damien's arms. "I shouldn't be here."

"No, you shouldn't." His mouth nipped at hers.

"We can't do this." Her hands slid under his sweater, caressing his slightly hairy chest. "This is madness."

"You're right." He groaned at her caresses and bit her earlobe in retaliation.

She closed her eyes briefly in ecstasy. "I…I should leave…" Her voice trailed off on a moan as he nipped at her jaw.

"Mmm-hmm," he murmured against her throat. "You really should."

Her hands moved up his strong arms to rest on his shoulders. She opened dazed eyes to stare into his ravenous ones.

"Damien, what are we doing?"

"Giving in to the inevitable."

His mouth took hers. Dear Lord in heaven, she was lost. He was right; this was inevitable. It was unwise; they shouldn't do it, but they could no more deny the wicked attraction between them than they could deny they needed oxygen to sustain their lives.

Words were forgotten as sure hands moved to her shoulders before sliding down her arms to the hem of her sweater. He slowly pulled the garment over her head. Hungry eyes feasted on the perfection of her exposed brown skin. Her hands took up residence under his sweater and she pulled it over his head, necessitating the removal of his hands from her for seconds, and then his fingertips lightly slid down the slopes of her firm, round breasts while his mouth found the pulse beating erratically at her neck before he lifted his head to fuse his lips with hers.

He kissed her senseless. His ravenous mouth opened wide over hers and demanded wholehearted participation from her, and she matched his ardor measure for measure. His tongue urgently caressed hers, and his hands roamed down her bare back to her hips, pressing her closer to his evident need. She sighed against his marauding lips, which after endless seconds, softened somewhat.

"I've wanted you since the second I laid eyes on you," he confessed against her mouth.

"You have?" Anxious fingers unsnapped his jeans and slid across his corrugated lower abdomen. "Really?"

For an answer, he picked her up effortlessly and laid her down on the bed, dispensing with her sweats and panties until she was finally lying naked before him. As he quickly removed his own clothing, their eyes drank their fill of each other's bodies. Reaching into the nightstand, he pulled out a condom, tore open the package and donned the protection before lying down beside her, pulling her into his aching arms and kissing her slowly yet passionately. She tasted smooth, silky and spicy. He could feast on her soft, full, addicting lips for hours and never get tired.

When he lifted his mouth from hers, she inhaled deeply before releasing her breath on a serrated moan when he purposefully bent his head and his hot mouth engulfed one of her firm breasts, giving it the same maddening attention to detail that he had her lips. His hand found her other breast, and her back arched off the bed as his teeth bit into a nipple made pebble hard by his wicked tongue and lips. She shuddered when he rubbed his hairy chin back and forth against the sensitized nubbin.

Pleading hands ran down his muscled arms and back as his scorching mouth snaked down her writhing body. She almost died on the spot as he, without asking permission, intimately familiarized himself with every inch of her. He pressed his parted lips against her soft, flat stomach, his rough tongue flirting inside her belly button before unhurriedly moving lower, leaving a trail of fire in its wake. Seeking fingers moved to her soft inner thighs, touching fleetingly several times before treating her to a longer caress as he stroked her intimately.

Her hands flew to the back of his head and held his

wicked mouth closer while he trailed wet kisses across her hips before following the path of his fingers to her inner thighs. She bit her lower lip, trying unsuccessfully to contain the groan of pleasure that erupted from her.

She was sweet, oh so sweet, and she completely and utterly owned him. The last rational thought that raced through his mind was that his wounded heart couldn't afford to get involved with her and risk injury again, but that sane thought was quickly dispersed by red-hot, maddening desire. He had to have her now; nothing else mattered.

Everywhere he touched, tiny fires flared until her entire body was a blazing inferno. His lips and hands easily melted the numbing cold indifference she had purposefully encased her heart in for years. She no longer cared what complete surrender would demand from her; only one thing mattered—appeasing the gnawing hunger that had resided in her since she had first danced with Damien.

"I want heat Tasha," he groaned against her flesh before his mouth continued its destructive path over her burning skin. "I want you to melt for me."

Her hands flew back and grasped the headboard as his tongue pierced her, feasted on her and had her bursting free until she knew nothing but carnal pleasure. She wasn't aware of anything for a few frenzied moments, and then his hard body covered hers; she felt his unbending naked flesh against her soft yielding form, and she knew she was about to truly blaze.

Without preamble, anxious hands parted her thighs and he at long last unerringly fused his body with hers. She arched up; her eyes flew open to meet the dark depths of his, and by mutual silent consent they began their long-denied dance of supreme passion.

God, he felt so wonderful, and he made her feel things she had only read about in books. She had never believed the pretty, sexy prose contained within romance novels, but now experiencing complete union with Damien, how could she not? With him, she was whole; her heartbeat synchronized with his, and she gave up any pretense that somewhere else other than right here, in his arms, was where she was meant to be. He had said he wanted heat, and she seared him and he her with the blinding ferocity of their too-long-denied passion.

He felt his lips tremble from the moan escaping from her throat, and he reluctantly released her mouth for a second so that the wonderful sound could fill his ears as he filled her body.

This was perfection. Her slender, strong limbs pulled him closer as she deliberately arched, taking him deeper and deeper. He wanted to ram himself into her, but he forced himself to take her in slow, long, maddening strokes.

They had both waited too long for this to rush it. He felt her trembling against him, and he almost went insane at the way she enveloped, accepted and vibrated in welcome around him. Oh, that he could stay this way with her forever—he would give up everything he owned if only he could.

The unbearable, agonizing pressure built within her with each silky kiss and every sensuous movement of his body against hers. She wanted to cry out in triumph and in frustration. He brought her to life with every forceful thrust, each heated kiss and maddening caress. She wanted to prolong the rapture, yet the tension had to be released soon or she would go mad.

"Tasha," he groaned against her neck over and over, and her bones melted at his use of the abbreviated form of her name—from now on, she silently vowed, no one would ever call her that except him.

His body began to move faster and harder against hers,

and she met each beautiful thrust, matched each deliberate movement. She allowed her passion-glazed mind to admit that she needed him more than anything else in the world. Her arms and body pulled him closer still. Her melting heart sung at the realization she was now completely his and he was hers. Then all semblance of rationality dissipated as she felt him shake violently against her and she began to shudder with him as they finally found blessed release and utter fulfillment.

When he could breathe again, he reluctantly shifted off her welcoming body and reclined on his back. Natasha turned onto her side and molded herself to him, laying her head on his shoulder. His fingers trailed down her arm to rest on her hip, before moving up her spine and then back down again.

Her fingers traced lazy circles on his smooth chest that her lips and tongue just had to imitate. She smiled when he groaned at her actions and the hand resting on her hip pulled her closer against him. For the first time in her life, she felt whole, completely relaxed and content.

She lightly ran her fingers up the faint two-inch scar on his right hip and similar vertical scar across his lower back.

"What happened here?" He tensed noticeably and she immediately regretted her question.

"Accident," he shortly replied.

She held back further questions and instead remained silent, caressing his back and kissing his chest until she felt him relax again. Obviously, it was a painful memory for him—one she hoped he would share with her in time.

They stayed that way a long time, not talking, but just touching, caressing and enjoying being so close. She never wanted to move again. How could one man encompass her entire world? She didn't know, but Damien did just that; that realization frightened her, but it also empowered her with a sense of belonging and peace unlike any she had ever known.

Natasha closed her eyes and pressed closer to Damien's slightly hairy chest, basking in the warm afterglow of their lovemaking. She would be content to never move from his strong arms.

"You haven't had many lovers, have you?"

Damien's out-of-the-blue inquiry elicited a gasp from her. "What?"

"You heard me." He tenderly stroked her back.

"Why are you asking me about that now?"

"I'm curious."

"Now?"

He chuckled softly. "Now's as good a time as any, don't you agree?"

She didn't. Frankly, she thought his timing stank.

"No, I don't."

"Tasha, come up here so I can see you."

"No." She resisted his efforts to bring them to eye level, burying her face in his chest instead.

He laughed softly and fingered her hair. "Don't get shy on me now."

"Why do you want to know about my past lovers?"

He tenderly answered, "Because it's obvious you haven't been with a lot of men."

"Oh." That tiny word encompassed a lot of emotion. "So you weren't satisfied?"

"I was very satisfied," he assured, adding arrogantly, "as were you."

"I was." Emboldened by his words, she kissed his chest.

"I know." He ran his palm down her back. "You were surprised by the amount of pleasure you experienced, which made me curious about your past lovers," he explained his previous question.

She found the courage to slide up against his body until her head lay beside his on the pillow. She didn't find smugness or condescension in his handsome face, which gave her the courage to answer his question. After the intimacies they had just shared, it was silly to feel shy with him now.

"I've had two lovers," she admitted on a sigh. "One was my high school boyfriend, who was my first."

"And the other?"

"A dancer." She lowered her eyes. "Four years ago."

"What happened?" He placed a hand under her chin, lifting her eyes to his again.

She shrugged. "In a nutshell, he was a lying, cheating asshole."

"What did he do to you?"

The concern in his eyes gave her the courage to continue. "He pretended to be interested in me."

"Pretended how?"

"What he really wanted was my nice Manhattan apartment in lieu of his Bronx basement, my huge bank account instead of his nonexistent one and the never-ending luxuries he expected me to constantly heap upon him instead of having to save all month just to afford eating out at a mediocre restaurant," she bitterly recounted.

"What a bastard!"

Her heart warmed at his vehement declaration. "He was absolutely."

"Tell me his name—" his eyes darkened dangerously "—and I'll take care of him for you."

"Damien, you will not," she laughingly admonished.

"Try me." He grinned, only half kidding.

"I appreciate the offer." She touched his face. "But I've long since forgotten about what's-his-name."

"I'm sorry that happened to you."

She shrugged. "It's all right. It was a valuable lesson."

"Yes." His eyes clouded. "The ones that hurt the most are the most valuable."

"Speaking from experience?"

"Definitely."

She kept her tone light. "Care to elaborate?"

"No." He reclined on his back. "Not really."

"Come on, Damien. I just bared my soul to you."

"And I appreciate it."

She supported herself on one elbow and glanced down at his unreadable expression as he stared at the ceiling. She wanted to press him but decided against it for now. She knew enough about Damien to realize it was hard for him to open up—even to a woman who had done just that to him. She understood keeping oneself closed off better than most.

Her fingers traced his furrowed brow. "Are you okay?"

"Yes." He laughed and gazed at her. "I'm fine."

"Good." She snuggled closer. They were silent for a few minutes, and her next words were spoken primarily to hear his response. "We shouldn't have let this happen."

"No, we shouldn't have. My number one rule is never to get involved with my employees."

Absurdly, his honest agreement wasn't what she wanted to hear—not while they lay so close that she could feel his heart beating against her. She lifted her head to gaze into his unreadable eyes.

"Then why are we here?"

"Pure animal lust is a very powerful thing."

"Lust?" She balked at his choice of words.

He trailed a finger down her cheek. "I've upset you."

"Why would that upset me?"

She tried to sound causal, but the hurt in her voice was clearly evident. Suddenly, she wished she could disappear.

"I'm just trying to be honest, Tasha."

"You have been." She averted her eyes. "I should go."

"Yes, you should."

She stiffened and tried to get out of bed; however, he placed an arm around her waist, pulling her back down to his side.

"How can I go if you won't release me?"

His arm tightened and he kissed her shoulder. "I said you should go, not that I wanted you to go."

"So, your lust hasn't been satisfied?"

"No," he smiled decadently. "Has yours?"

"I don't want to play games with you, Damien."

"Neither do I." He nibbled at her collarbone.

"This was a mistake." She tried unsuccessfully to free herself. "Let's not prolong it."

He turned her onto her back. "It may be a mistake, but I definitely want to prolong it. Don't you?"

"Damien…" Her voice trailed off as he cupped a breast.

"Yes." He smiled, whisking his thumb across her nipple.

"Stop that."

"Stop what?" His thumb continued to rub her nipple maddeningly. "This?"

"Yes." She sighed breathily.

"You sure about that?"

"Yes, I… Oh!" His mouth took the place of his hand for several tantalizing moments.

"Let's throw caution to the wind and break the rules one more time, Tasha."

She didn't get the chance to agree or disagree, because his focused body covered hers and his seeking mouth sank into hers, effectively silencing any response she might make.

An hour later, Natasha sat on the edge of the rumpled bed wearing one of Damien's T-shirts. He was in the kitchen preparing an after-midnight snack. She silently prayed morning would never come because when it did, reality would rear its ugly head. She glanced at the clock; it was a little before two and she would have to return to her room soon, but not quite yet. They still had a little time together as a man and a woman.

She smiled as Damien entered the bedroom with a tray in his hands. His black robe was opened down to his stomach. Her heart lurched at the sight of him so devilishly handsome, so decadently desirable, and for tonight he was one hundred percent hers.

His eyes intercepted her appreciative gaze and he smiled. Without hesitation, he placed the tray on the bedside table and pulled her into his arms.

"Damien…" she whispered in slight protest. "I'm hungry."

His mouth covered hers hotly, sweetly, effectively silencing her. She felt his fingers insinuating beneath her shirt and easily pulling it off. Despite her declaration of hunger, eager fingers undid his robe and pushed it off his broad shoulders until it joined her shirt. Their limbs entangled intimately as mouths and tongues mated wildly.

"I'm hungry too." Purposeful hands lifted her hips until he filled her. "Ravenous."

She groaned against his mouth, "Take me now."

Food was forgotten, everything was forgotten except this never-ending need they had for each other that would no longer be denied.

Much later, Natasha nibbled on Damien's neck. "This is heaven."

"You won't get an argument from me." His hand went behind her head, holding her wandering mouth closer. "Tasha, that feels so good," he whispered against her ear.

"How good?" Her voice was muffled by his flesh.

"Very."

After several more nibbles at his skin, she pulled back slightly. "We really should talk seriously, I suppose."

His fingers ran through her soft hair, drawing her lips inexorably toward his waiting, hungry ones. He loved the feel of every inch of her against every corresponding part of him. Suddenly his fingers froze and his entire body tensed.

Natasha stared into his stressed face. "What's the matter, Damien?"

He sighed before admitting, "It just occurred to me that I forgot to use a condom the last time."

"It's all right," she assured him. "I'm on the pill."

His features relaxed considerably. "I shouldn't have been so careless."

"Why were you?"

"Because—" appreciative eyes traversed her beautiful face "—I couldn't wait to get my hands on you."

"That's a good reason," she approved.

"I'm usually very conscientious about using protection."

"I believe you."

"You make me lose control—completely."

"Ditto." They were quiet for a while before she asked, "Damien, what are we going to do?"

She didn't want to bring this up now, but they did need to talk. They had to think about how they were going to act around the rest of the troupe now that they were no longer only employer and employee.

He sighed. "This ballet is important to both of us."

"It is, yes."

"Then I suggest we keep our new relationship between us. When we're at work, we keep it strictly professional."

"And when we're not at work?" She held her breath, waiting for his response.

"Let's play it by ear."

It wasn't exactly what she wanted to hear, but given their precarious situation, his suggestion made sense. At least he wasn't thanking her for a one-night stand and making her feel as if she had only been a pleasant diversion.

"Okay."

"Okay," he whispered into her mouth as his body covered hers.

Efficient hands quickly parted the sheet, and his body took what he wanted and gave them both what they needed.

Chapter 8

Damien reclined against the headboard with Natasha lying against his chest. He couldn't remember ever feeling more contented.

"Thanksgiving is almost here."

"Yes, it is." Natasha snuggled closer to him. "It can't get here soon enough for me. I can't wait to have a few days off."

"Sick of work already?"

"No, not at all." She laughed. "It is just that I can't wait to see my family. There is nothing like family for the holidays."

"Agreed." His fingers trailed across her shoulder. "My parents and sister are going to Washington to visit my uncle."

She tilted her head to stare at him. "Are you going with them?"

"No, I have too much to do and too little time to do it in."

"Can't you at least take one day off?"

"Don't worry about me," he laughingly ordered.

"I'm not," she quickly denied, but she didn't like the prospect of him spending the holiday alone.

"Good. They'll be back soon enough, and they're coming to the premiere. Are your folks still planning on attending?"

"Wild horses couldn't keep them and Nicole away, but I don't know about Nathan. We haven't seen him in four years."

"Why so long?"

"He works for the State Department as a lawyer and is always in one faraway place or another." She shrugged. "His career is very important to him."

"It's a family trait, I see."

She frowned. "What do you mean?"

"Just that work is primary in both of your lives."

"Yes, it has been."

"Has been?" He watched her closely.

"It is," she quickly amended.

"All work and no play..."

"Makes Natasha a prepared ballerina," she smilingly finished.

"You're an excellent ballerina."

"Thank you." She kissed his chest lingeringly before reluctantly moving out of his arms and getting out of bed before he could stop her.

"What are you doing?"

"Dressing." She bent down and picked up her hastily discarded clothes.

"I can see that." He sat up. "Why?"

"Because I can't go back to my room naked, can I?"

"Mmm." His eyes traveled over her bare body. "I don't mind."

"Well, I don't want to flash anyone else."

"You'd better not." He threw back the covers. "It's true what they say, isn't it?"

Her toes curled at the possessiveness of his voice. Her eyes dilated at the sight of his splendidly naked body as he got out of bed and took her into his arms.

"What do they say?"

"Time flies—" his fingers entangled in her hair, pulling her head aback "—when you're experiencing multiple orgasms."

"Yes," she said and laughed throatily. "It certainly does."

"Wanna have some more of this type of fun tomorrow night?"

"I think—" she nibbled at his mouth "—that can be arranged."

"Good." He kissed her silly.

"I'm not sorry, Damien," she vowed against his lips.

"Neither am I."

She smiled and kissed him briefly before moving out of his arms and going back to her room to get a few hours of sleep before their very early day began.

The next morning when Damien and Natasha saw each other at rehearsal, it was business as usual. They both acted appropriately, but Rachel sensed a tangible change in her partner.

"What's up with you, old friend?"

"Nothing." He glanced at her as she sat on a stool beside him, a short distance from the stage.

"Nothing?" Rachel studied his smiling profile. "Why are you so…giddy?"

Damien arched an eyebrow. "I've never been giddy a day in my life."

Rachel laughed. "Okay, maybe that was the wrong word. How about cheerful?"

"Is it a crime to be cheerful, Rachel?"

"No, of course it isn't."

"Natasha, try that combination again," Damien's voice rang out. "I want the pirouettes crisper."

From the stage, a smiling Natasha nodded, waited for the music to start again and began dancing as instructed. His eyes never left his ballerina's, and he felt Rachel's speculative gaze continuing to rest on him.

"That was better, but not great. Try it again."

"Yes, sir." Natasha acquiesced and started dancing once more.

"So." Rachel stared at his profile. "What did you do last night?"

"Slept, Mom." He continued watching Natasha dance. "And you?"

Rachel laughed. "The same."

"That's it, Natasha," Damien finally approved. "Dennis, try it with her."

He watched her and her partner dance close, and a streak of jealously shot through him, which he quickly tamped down. She had been in his bed last night and would be again tonight. She didn't want Dennis, and he had to keep his mind on the ballet; his personal feelings for Natasha had no place in this rehearsal hall. Despite his silent dressing down, he paused—his *personal feelings* for Natasha? Not his *desire* for her? Desire he could deal with, but *feelings?* Oh, damn.

"Damien?"

He briefly glanced at Rachel. "What?"

Rachel frowned. "Where were you?"

He scratched his hair-covered chin. "Right here."

"You seemed miles away."

"Just concentrating on Natasha and Dennis."

"Yes." Rachel smiled knowingly. "I can see that."

"Rachel…" The way he said her name held a warning.

"Save your bark for someone who cares." Rachel laughed. "I've known you too long, and I know something is definitely going on with you."

"You have known me a long time," he agreed. "Long enough to know when you're getting on my nerves."

Rachel's spontaneous resounding laughter caused heads to turn in their direction. Damien's shoulders noticeably tightened in irritation.

"And you've known me long enough to know that I don't stop until I learn what I want to know," she smilingly countered when he refused to look at her. "Come on, Damien, tell me about it."

He frowned. "Tell you about what?"

"What's causing the change in you—or rather, whom?" When he remained silent, she hypothesized, "Is it Natasha?"

"What does she have to do with anything?"

"I think she has everything to do with the change I sense in you." She paused thoughtfully before continuing, "You're different since meeting her."

"That's nonsense. I'm the same as I've always been."

"No." She glanced at his frowning profile thoughtfully. "You're happier."

"Of course I'm happy, Rachel." He spared her a brief, irritated glance. "My ballet is cast, rehearsals are coming along nicely and…"

"You've met Natasha," she finished for him.

"She's just a ballerina. Nothing more."

Before she could continue her inquisition, he stood and walked toward the stage. He was surprised a bolt of lightning didn't strike him after the out-and-out lie he had just told his best friend—because the one thing Natasha wasn't was just another ballerina.

* * *

Natasha tightened the belt of her short pink robe before slowly opening the door to her room. Her heartbeat intensified and every nerve ending in her body stood at attention when she saw who was on the other side—although she had instinctively known the identity of her late-night caller before opening the door.

"Damien," she whispered. "What are you doing here?"

"What do you think?"

He curved a possessive arm around her waist, pressed his mouth to hers and ushered her back inside her room, closing the door behind them. She unbuttoned his shirt and spread her fingers over his tempting, muscled chest. He smiled against her mouth and his tongue sought and found hers, engaging in a slow, sensual duel that intensified the gnawing ache within their lower bodies.

"You shouldn't be here," she weakly protested when he released her clinging lips.

"Why not?" His hands ran down her back to her hips, pressing her closer.

"Because—" she sighed at his actions "—it's too dangerous."

"No more so than it was last night."

"You know what I mean." She ineffectively pushed at his solid shoulders. "Will you stop it?"

His answer was to pull her closer as his fingers maddeningly dug into the soft flesh of her butt. She closed her eyes briefly against the torrential desire flowing through her veins like molten hot lava.

"You don't want me to."

"Yes, I…"

His hot mouth silenced the rest of her ridiculous words. The ensuing kiss was completely, wonderfully carnal and singed them both to the core of their beings. Her arms encircled his neck, and she sensually moved her body against his. In response, his mouth opened wider, forcing hers to do the same as the kiss escalated to inferno status. His hands moved to her waist, loosening the belt of her robe and spreading apart the satiny folds so that eager fingers could investigate the warm, responsive flesh beneath. She moaned against his persuasive lips and surrendered to heaven for a few minutes until a knock sounded at her door, followed by another and another still.

"Damn," he groaned against her sweet mouth, "don't answer it."

"I have to." She pushed out of his arms and placed a hand over her thoroughly kissed lips. "Stay behind the door, and please keep quiet."

"Don't answer it," he whispered in her ear as his arms went around her from behind.

"Damien, stop." She sighed, moved out of his arms, re-adjusted her robe and carefully turned the doorknob, opening the door slightly.

"Hi, Natasha. Wanna join a group of us for drinks by the fireplace downstairs?" Simone asked.

"Uh, no." She fought to suppress a moan as Damien kissed her neck and nibbled at her earlobe. "I'm beat."

Thankfully, Damien stayed behind the door and out of Simone's view. His actions, however, were destroying her ability to reason. She bit her lower lip and clinched the doorknob tighter when his fingers wandered under the hem of her robe to touch her inner thigh, sliding upward suggestively.

"Are you okay?" Simone stared at her intently.

"Hmm?" Natasha elbowed Damien in the stomach before firmly asserting, "Yeah, I'm fine. Just tired. Tell everyone I'll see them tomorrow."

She reached behind her and removed Damien's hand from her breast. "I'm just going to crawl into bed and sleep."

"Okay." Simone smiled. "See you in the morning. Night."

"Good night."

She had no sooner closed the door than Damien's body pressed her back against it and his mouth captured hers again. His body molded against hers so perfectly that she couldn't discern where he ended and she began. It should be a first-degree crime for a man to be so sexy and make her want him so much.

"Damien, shame on you." She placed hands on her hips. "You know we can't be seen together."

"I know. I'm just a bad boy." He lowered his head to sample her soft neck. "What are you going to do with me?"

"I have a mind to…" She closed her eyes as desire washed over her.

"To what?" His voice was muffled against her fragrant skin. "Mmm, you smell good."

"You feel good." Her hands ran up and down his muscled chest.

"I know something that feels even better."

"Yeah?" She backed against the door. "Show me."

"With pleasure."

Hungry lips closed possessively over hers, successfully ending any further conversation. Searching hands pulled her silk robe completely apart as he simultaneously backed her into a nearby wall. Fingers trailed across and cupped her breasts, stroking and teasing until she was writhing against him. His hands grabbed hers and directed them to the fly of his jeans, which anxious fingers quickly unzipped, and then together they slid the material down his hips and sheathed him in a condom. His seeking body pressed against and conformed to hers. Strong hands lifted her legs off the floor, hooking them around his waist, and then he plunged into her.

She cried out in shocked pleasure against his hardening lips as he ravaged her. As he intended, talk was forgotten; everything was forgotten as he filled her body, soul and heart. Her arms and legs held him tight as his body took hers intimately. Her eyes closed and she moaned against his mouth. Their desire built and peaked with every movement, every jagged breath until it broke free like water bursting forth from a dam, flooding their hearts and senses with indescribable pleasure, until they were both willingly drowning in a pool of unparalleled hedonistic bliss.

Several hours later, Natasha and Damien lay close on the bed, limbs intimately entwined. She still didn't understand how one man could give her everything she needed, but somehow he did. That simple fact frightened and elated her. How had he become so important to her in such a short time, and what was she going to do about her increasing addiction to him and the threat it posed to her career?

She wished she could stay in his arms all night, but logically she knew she couldn't. He had to return to his room so that they could snatch a few hours of uninterrupted sleep before rehearsals tomorrow. Sighing resignedly, she kissed his chest lingeringly before rolling away from him.

"Where are you going?" He missed her warmth as she got out of bed and donned her robe.

"Nowhere." She pulled back the cover to reveal his magnificent body and willed her eyes to focus on his face. "But you have to go back to your room."

He stood. "Why?"

She glanced at the clock that glared out 3:05 a.m. Damn time for refusing to stand still. She didn't want him to leave her, but they couldn't be found together.

"Because we need to be up soon for rehearsal."

She tried to sidestep him, but his arms went around her and pressed her close to his naked body. His lips made a beeline for and played with hers.

"Damien." Her hands rested on his hard shoulders. "Let me go."

"Is that what you really want?" he asked against her ear.

"No," she moaned softly, then more forcefully, "but you know we can't be found together."

"I know."

His mouth sought out hers, but she pushed away from him and took a step back before he could reach his destination.

She bent down, retrieved his pants and handed them to him. He reluctantly pulled on his pants and walked toward her again.

"Kiss me good-night, Tasha."

"Damien…" She shook her head in remonstration at his innocent expression.

"Really, just a kiss. I won't even touch you." To prove his point, he placed his hands behind his back.

"All right," she smilingly relented, "but then you have to go."

"I promise." He crossed his heart and then returned his hand behind his back.

She took a step toward him and placed her hands on his slightly stubbly cheeks, rose up on her tiptoes and brought her mouth into contact with his. She only meant to kiss him lightly, but one touch of his addictive, responsive lips had her leaning into his hard body and going deep and deeper still until she was kissing him lingeringly, achingly, as if she would never stop; long seconds later she reluctantly ended contact and stepped away from temptation.

Despite the desire rocketing through him, as promised,

he didn't touch her. His chest rose rapidly with the effort he was exerting to control himself and keep his hands off her. Neither of them spoke for a few seconds—simply stared longingly at each other, their mutual desire speaking louder than any words. Somehow she tore her eyes away from his, walked to the door, carefully opened it and peered outside before motioning to him.

"Good night."

He smiled at her actions. "Good night, Tasha."

He walked through the door without touching her and padded silently down the hallway to his room. Her sad eyes stared after him before she resolutely closed the door and leaned against it, employing every ounce of self-control not to run after him and ask him to stay with her—something she knew he couldn't do.

Once alone, Natasha sank down onto the bed and curled her legs underneath her, chewing on her lower lip contemplatively. Since she and Damien had finally given in to the inescapable desire, where did they go from here? They wanted each other, that much was certain, yet were they building something tangible, or simply enjoying the here and now? Which did she want—the former or the latter?

Her career was finally going the way she wanted, and she should be concentrating on that—and she was; however, she now also wanted something else in addition to fame—a chance to see where whatever this was she had begun with Damien was heading. What did Damien want? Would their journey from this point on be together, or would they soon part and go their separate ways? That was the problem— she had a million questions and not a single answer.

Chapter 9

A week later, they returned to the hustle of New York. Since the retreat, Natasha and Damien had grown closer, and for the first time she was seriously contemplating trying to juggle a romantic relationship alongside her career.

After an unusually grueling day of rehearsals, Natasha tiredly reached her apartment around 8:45 p.m. As she exited the elevator, she wished she had taken Damien up on his dinner invitation. This was the first night they were spending apart in eight days, and she missed him already. *Idiot, you can do without him for one night.* Lord knows the rest would do them both good.

Sighing, she turned the key to unlock the door and stopped in her tracks when she found the object of her thoughts, Damien, dressed in a meticulous navy suit and standing beside an elegantly set candlelit table for two.

"What are you doing here?"

"Since it would be unwise for us to be seen in a restaurant—" he smiled "—I thought I'd surprised you with a gourmet dinner here."

She dropped her gym bag onto a chair and pulled the band from her hair. His elegant attire made her all the more conscious of her own shabby dress of sweats and sneakers.

"You definitely surprised me." She dropped her keys on the table and approached him. "Is this why you had Rachel take over the last hour of rehearsal?"

He grinned. "Yeah, I had to get my surprise ready."

Natasha echoed his smile. "How did you get in here?"

"I bribed the super."

"You didn't." She shook her head reproachfully.

"Oh yes, I did."

She chuckled. "How much did it cost you?"

"I'm not telling." He kissed her lingeringly. "It might make you too conceited."

"Mmm." She wound her arms around his neck. "Maybe I should give you a key so you won't have to resort to such drastic measures again."

She held her breath and waited for his response to her spontaneous offer. She hadn't meant to say that, but she meant it nonetheless. She stared unwaveringly into his intense eyes as he contemplated her words.

"Maybe you should," he spoke after several seconds of contemplative silence.

She sighed inwardly at his agreement, glad she hadn't freaked him out. They smiled at each other before their mouths met in a searing, thorough kiss. Natasha's face registered surprise when he pulled back.

"Now go and change." He pushed her toward the bedroom. "You'll find everything you need laid out on your bed."

"What have you done?" She laughed and walked toward the bedroom.

"You'll see."

In her room she found a gorgeous white sleeveless gown and matching pumps. She fingered the sheer, expensive fabric and shook her head in wonder before traipsing happily into the bathroom to shower.

About half an hour later, she emerged wearing the figure-hugging gown that accentuated all of her curves and drew attention to her rounded breasts. She left her hair loose and flowing the way he liked it.

His mouth dropped open at her entrance. Gazing at the beauty before him, he felt as if he had been punched hard in the stomach. Damn, she was beautiful, and he was completely enthralled by her. After several silent, electric seconds, he walked over and took her hand.

"You look like a goddess." He handed her a single white rose.

"Thank you." She sniffed her flower and ran a hand down her hip. "This gown is exquisite."

He shook his head. "It was just an old scrap until you put it on. You make the gown, not the other way around."

She basked in his warm, appreciative gaze. "Thank you."

"You're welcome." He kissed the back of her hand.

"How did you know my size?"

"Natasha—" he grinned wickedly "—I've explored every inch of you. There's nothing about your body that I don't know."

Her mouth dropped open in shock, and he laughed at her obvious discomfiture. He placed a hand under her chin and kissed her briefly.

"Shall we eat?"

"Yes." She found her voice again and followed him to the table and sat down in the chair he held out for her. "This is too much."

"You're too much." He poured her some champagne and raised his glass in a toast. "To us."

"To us," she smilingly echoed.

They ate the wonderful lobster dinner he had ordered from one of the most expensive restaurants in the city with gusto. Laughing, touching and gazing at each other anticipatorily were things they did frequently during their delicious meal.

"When did you have time to do all of this?"

"That's my secret." He added with a wink, "Just as long as you're sufficiently impressed."

"Oh, I definitely am." She laughed and then sobered. "You're too good to me."

Intense eyes locked on hers. "Am I good for you?"

"Yes." She released her breath silently. "Yes, I think you are."

He smiled in approval. "Dance with me."

"I'd love to." She took his hand, stood and went willingly into his arms.

The soft romantic music that filled the air was another layer to the sexual excitement that was steadily developing within them. Each knew it would soon have to be released, and they anticipated that culminating moment as much as they were savoring the delicious buildup to it.

She inhaled deeply. He smelled wonderfully of expensive cologne and his own unique scent that she had rapidly become accustomed to. She had no doubt she could find him in the dark easily. Their bodies fit perfectly together—she couldn't wait to get as close to him as humanly possible. She ached for him with her heart, body and soul.

The hands on her waist moved lower to her hips, pulling her so tight that she felt every hard inch of him, especially the bulge in his groin. Her eyes darkened to match his as they barely moved. One of her hands stroked the back of his neck, eliciting a growl from deep within him; she smiled and pressed enticingly closer while simultaneously biting his lower lip and pulling it into her hungry mouth.

He easily picked her up until her feet dangled in midair and fused his mouth with hers. The kiss they shared was hot, heavy and illicit. They tilted their heads this way and then that as they deepened the kiss to the point of complete incineration. They both were trembling when their lips broke contact long minutes later.

"Natasha, I want you," he growled against her mouth.

"How much?"

"Want me to show you?"

"Yes." She sighed the word and wound her arms tighter around his neck. "I don't want this night to end."

"Who says it has to?" He softly kissed her sweet lips.

"Stay with me." Her eyes pleaded with his.

"Do you really think—" he kissed her soundly "—I planned to leave you tonight?"

"I'd kill you if you did."

He smiled at her whispered threat, picked her up and carried her into the bedroom. He sat her down by the bed, and their mouths drifted together. Sure hands connected with and slowly pulled down the zipper of her dress and pulled the now-offensive material from her until she was naked in his arms. He released her mouth and pulled back slightly to stare at her perfect milk chocolate flesh. A finger slowly encircled a hard nipple, and at her quick indrawn breath, his thumb rubbed across the protruding peak.

Her fingers easily dispensed with his tie, shirt and jacket before moving to his belt and zipper of his pants. She was trembling with anticipation when at long last they stood before each other without the distasteful barrier of their clothing. As he leisurely caressed her breasts, her fingers danced across his muscled chest before sliding low to his corrugated stomach and lower still until, hot and hard, he filled her hands. She tortured him with ardent caresses before his hands pushed hers aside to put on a condom.

Suddenly they were on the bed and his body was pressing hers into the mattress. His mouth engulfed hers while his fingers entwined with hers, and he easily kept her hands anchored above her head while he excruciatingly, slowly joined their burning bodies into one.

She pulled against his fingers, but he refused to release her hands, holding her captive, preventing her from touching him. She whimpered against his mouth, her body arched against his supreme hardness, and she fought to maintain her sanity.

He was intent on making slow, maddening love to her. His powerful body stroked her straining one slowly, refusing to be rushed by her or by the gnawing hunger consuming them. She tried again to free her hands, but his response was to tighten his grip on her fingers.

"I want you to go insane with me," he whispered into her mouth. "Absolutely, completely insane."

She was already there; couldn't he tell? It was maddening and exhilarating being unable to caress him with her hands, and so she settled on using the contracting walls of her body to drive him to a fever pitch that had him hoarsely crying out as he lowered her arms to each side of her head, his fingers still clasped around hers. She thought she would go stark, raving mad from the exquisite slow torture and the unparalleled pleasure he subjected her to—and she did long minutes later; he joined her as their bodies began to shake violently for suspended minutes before finally stilling as rapturous release thundered through them.

His head rested in the crook of her neck. Her hands now free, fingers strummed down his spine, eliciting an incoherent groan and spasmodic tremor from her lover. She smiled contentedly and held him close as their breathing slowly returned to normal.

She had never felt so cherished or special. He had just taken a huge chunk of her previously guarded heart tonight, and there was absolutely nothing she could have done to stop him; she hadn't even wanted to try.

They fell asleep in each other's arms, completely content and absolutely satisfied.

Natasha hadn't seen Damien since he had forced himself to leave her arms several hours ago back at her apartment. They had shared a wonderfully romantic night—one neither had wanted to end. Inevitably, though, a new day had dawned, sending them back into their roles of employee and employer, which both knew were necessary yet were beginning to resent. It was four-thirty in the morning, and she hadn't seen Damien on her way into the building; she wondered if he was here yet.

Natasha smiled dreamily as she remembered the magical time she and Damien had spent together. When she entered the practice room, she was met by Erina who quickly sent her into her morning workout routine.

"Natasha!" Erina's sharp voice rang out when she stumbled.

"I'm sorry." Natasha tucked a stray strand of hair behind her ear.

Erina sighed. "Concentration, Natasha. Where is your mind?"

"I guess I'm not fully awake yet."

"Then I will just have to work you harder to shake off, how do you say, the cobwebs," Erina darkly promised.

Natasha's mouth set in determination. "I'm focused now."

"We shall see."

Natasha sighed at Erina's stern tones informing that her

coach wasn't happy with her at the moment. With much effort, Natasha forced her thoughts away from Damien and focused on following Erina's instructions.

"Very good, Natasha," Erina approved fifteen minutes later. "Now you are concentrating."

"I told you I would." Natasha wiped perspiration from her forehead with the back of her hand and glanced toward the open door.

"Why do you keep looking at the door?"

"I'm not," Natasha quickly denied.

"Are you expecting for someone?"

"No."

"Mr. Johnson seems taken with you."

Erina's out-of-the-blue comment took Natasha completely by surprise. Natasha was careful to keep her expression blank when she turned to face the keen eyes of her coach.

"Does he?" She fought to hide her pleasure at her observation. "I hadn't noticed."

"I see my observation pleases you."

"No, I…" Natasha paused and changed course. "Well, of course I want him to be happy with my dancing."

"Of course." Erina continued to watch her closely. "You seem different, Natasha."

"I do?" Natasha deliberately sat on the floor and stretched until her hands were touching her toes, forcing her eyes from her coach's perceptive ones. "How?"

"You're more comfortable in your skin, carefree and happier than I have ever seen you."

"Of course I am." Natasha rose with both arms stretched high above her head, eyes focused on the ceiling. "I'm finally going to dance the lead. I'm a part of a world-famous company and…"

"You have met Mr. Johnson."

Natasha lowered her arms and performed waist stretches to the right and then to the left sides. "That wasn't what I was going to say."

"No?" Erina watched her closely. "It is the truth, though, is it not?"

"Of course I'm glad I met Damien." Natasha chose her words carefully. "He's giving me my big break."

"True, but his main effect on you has been personal instead of professional, no?"

Natasha avoided her mentor's keen eyes and stretched down again. "I don't know what you mean."

"Then I will spell it out for you. You are interested in him."

"No, I'm not." Her denial rang out quickly—a little too quickly to be believed, especially by someone who knew her as well as Erina did.

"You do not have to lie to me."

"I'm not. I…"

"Look at me," Erina softly ordered and smiled lovingly when Natasha slowly complied. "You are like my daughter. I have known you almost your entire life, you cannot fool me."

"I know." She smiled softly.

"Then why are you trying to?" Erina chided. "Tell me what is going on with you."

"Damien and I are…friends."

"There are friends, and there are friends."

"Erina, my feelings for Damien are appropriate."

She prayed her coach would leave it at that. Of course, she didn't.

"Natasha." Erina sat down beside her and placed a hand on her arm. "You have worked so hard to achieve the success that is within your grasp now."

"I have." She nodded positively.

"Don't throw it all away by crossing a line that you know should not be crossed."

It was way too late for that piece of advice. However, she didn't tell Erina that—though she sensed the wise woman was aware of that fact.

"I appreciate your advice, Erina. You know that."

"I do." Erina squeezed her hand comfortingly before continuing, "I know Mr. Johnson is a handsome, fascinating man."

"But?"

"But—" she patted both her hands "—There is no room for two great passions in a ballerina's life."

"I know," Natasha softly agreed. "I know."

She unblinkingly met the concern in Erina's eyes. She was right, and she knew it. She knew what she should do, but for once in her life, it contradicted mightily with what she wanted to do.

Natasha entered her apartment and sank wearily down onto the sofa. Damien had been an absolute taskmaster today, and she had loved every second of it. He never let any of his dancers get away with being mediocre or lazy— a fact she absolutely applauded him for. She had learned more working with him the past weeks than she had in years with other directors, and she was without a doubt a much better dancer and person because of him.

She stretched out her legs and plopped her aching feet down on the glass table in front of the sofa, sighing wearily. As soon as she could move, she planned a hot bath and then a date with her warm, inviting bed. She and Damien weren't seeing each other tonight, and frankly, tired as she was, she wished they were; she had quickly become an addict where he was concerned, but it was an addiction she would happily never break. She smiled, stretched her arms over her head and closed her eyes as memories of the sweet, scandalous night she and Damien had shared last night washed over her.

She jumped at the sudden ringing of the doorbell and sprinted to open it. A welcoming smile lit up her face as she flung the door open, expecting to find Damien, but instead she received the surprise of her life.

"Nicole!" Natasha squealed in joy, enfolding her sister in a warm embrace.

They were the same height and coloring, though Nicole's shape was a bit more curvaceous than was Natasha's. They had often been mistaken for twins, although Nicole was two years her junior.

"Hi, sis." Nicole squeezed her hard.

"What are you doing here?" Natasha pulled her inside.

"I couldn't wait to see you." Nicole took off her hat and coat and placed them over a chair. "I decided to come into Manhattan, do some shopping and surprise you."

"I'm so glad you did." Natasha affectionately took her sister's hands in hers. Her eyes widened as they beheld the short tresses curling attractively around her sister's face. "Nicole, your hair!"

"Please, don't mention it." Nicole shook her head in exasperation. "Momma still almost cries every time she sees me."

"I like it." Natasha ran fingers through the short locks that framed her angelic face.

"Really?" Nicole self-consciously touched the hair at her nape. "So do I. Who needs all that hair?"

"It looks great. Don't worry about Momma. She'll get used to it. After all, it is your hair."

"Tell that to her." Nicole sighed expressively.

Natasha chuckled in sympathy. "Momma will be Momma."

"How about going out for a fancy dinner, or are you too tired?" For the first time, she noticed her sister was dressed in her leotards and baggy sweatpants.

"Too tired to share good food that I don't have to cook and conversation with you? Never." Natasha negatively shook her head. "Give me twenty minutes to shower and change."

"Fine. I'll call Momma and let her know that I haven't met a horrible fate for the few hours I've been here."

They both laughed, and then Natasha excused herself to go and get ready.

Forty minutes later, Natasha and Nicole were seated in a restaurant, sitting close, whispering like children.

"So, Tash." Nicole sipped her water. "Tell me about this new man in your life."

"What new man?" Natasha slowly countered.

"The one who has placed this infectious smile on your lips." Nicole pinched her cheek playfully. "You haven't stopped smiling yet."

Natasha's smile widened. "Is it a crime to be happy?"

"No, but you're always so serious. Happiness suits you, and I have a hunch a man is responsible for at least part of the change I sense in you."

"I can never fool you." Natasha chuckled happily.

"Then stop trying."

"I'm seeing someone. Damien—my boss." Natasha admitted the latter on a whisper.

Nicole's eyes dilated in shock. "Your boss?"

"Yes." Natasha nodded. "I know, I know."

"Tash." Nicole squeezed her hand. "Do you know what you're doing?"

"For the first time in my life relationshipwise, I think I do."

"How did this happen?"

"I don't know." Natasha shook her head in awe. "It was the last thing I expected, but, Nicole, I—he's just wonderful."

"Tell me about him," Nicole invited.

"First of all, he gave me the chance no one else would."

"I know you, Tash. Damien didn't *give* you anything. You *earned* this role with hard work, dedication and persistence."

"Thanks."

"I know you're grateful to him, but maybe…"

"I am," Natasha interrupted, paused meaningfully and assured, "but not *that* grateful. My feelings for Damien began as admiration and quickly changed to like. From the moment I met him, there was a spark of attraction between us. I didn't intend to act on it and neither did he, but we couldn't ignore our feelings—and believe me, we tried."

Nicole shook her head. "This is so unlike you, Tash."

"I know it is, but with Damien…" She paused, searching for the right words. "Nicole, I feel whole with him. He makes me want to enjoy life, and, more importantly, he accepts me for me."

"Accepts you how?"

"You know having money has been a huge obstacle in getting people to take me seriously as a dancer." At Nicole's nod, she continued, "Damien doesn't think I'm playing at being a ballerina the way so many others have. Without hesitation, he believed this part meant everything to me. I didn't have to waste my breath trying to convince him of my dedication to dancing—he just *knew*. He doesn't expect any special favors from me in return for the wonderful opportunity he's given me—except devotion to the dance. He works me until I want to cry uncle, so much so that sometimes I want to murder him." She laughed and Nicole joined her. "He just lets me be me, Nicole. I don't have to pretend with him at all."

Nicole couldn't help but smile at her sister's radiant expression. "How long has this been going on?"

"A few weeks. I know you're thinking I'm rushing into this, but you know me, Nicole, I never rush into anything. I understand your concern. I share it, but if I could go back and change anything, I wouldn't. Damien has taught me so much about myself and how to appreciate life."

"In a few short weeks?"

"In a few short weeks," Natasha assured. "We went ice skating, and Damien soon had everyone on the rink skating with us, playing silly games—in all the times I've skated in public, I've never done that before, and it was so much fun." She chuckled at the memory. "We were pair skating and suddenly he stopped and kissed me right there in front of everybody and, Nicole, it was…"

"Fabulous," Nicole smilingly supplied.

"Yes, it was—earth-shattering. I know that sounds cliché, but it was. That was such a magical night for me."

"I can see that in your face." Nicole touched her hand. "Tell me more."

"After that, we both tried to ignore what had happened—tried to go back to being employer and employee. We held out for weeks until our retreat in Saratoga Springs. There, he taught me to ride a horse and we had a full-fledged snowball fight." She laughed out loud. "We played like children and ended up lying in the snow, and we kissed again." She closed her eyes briefly. "After that, everything changed between us—for the better."

"Well—" Nicole sipped her coffee "—this is serious, isn't it?"

"I think it could be."

"I'm happy for you, Tash," Nicole stated. "But your boss?

That could open a messy can of worms if you're not careful."

"I know—we know." Natasha acknowledged on a sigh. "No one is aware that we're…dating. We keep things strictly professional when we're at work."

"And how's that working out?"

"Perfectly so far, and I pray it continues that way." Natasha crossed two fingers. "Nicole, I tried not to feel anything for him, really I did, but I couldn't help it. I like him—a lot."

"And how does he feel about you?"

Her smile brightened. "He likes me too."

"What about the future? Where do you see the two of you going from here?"

"I'm not worrying about the future." Natasha's response was lightly delivered and completely untrue. "For once in my life, I'm just going to enjoy the here and now."

Nicole frowned. "And that's enough for you?"

"Yes, it is."

"Really, Tash?" Nicole studied her sister closely. "You don't sound like a woman engaged in a casual affair."

"I'm happy, Nicole." Natasha sidestepped her sister's keen observation. "I'm really happy."

"I can see you are, but your feelings for Damien run deep. I don't want you to be hurt."

"I won't be. Everything I've worked so hard for is within my reach now, and I've met a wonderful man. I just want to enjoy…" Natasha's words halted and she almost dropped her fork back into her plate as Damien strolled into the restaurant with a gorgeous brunette on his arm.

She unsuccessfully fought to keep her mouth from dropping open as she watched them seated across the room, almost hidden by stray leaves and branches of various plants. Who was that woman? Who was that breathtakingly beautiful woman, she grudgingly amended.

Whoever the woman was, they seemed to like each other very, very much. When he leaned close and whispered something into her diamond-studded ear, the woman burst into laughter before lightly tapping his cheek in reproof. Damien kissed her cheek and smiled at her as if he adored her.

She felt rage slowly building within her. She knew she should look away before he saw her, but her eyes refused to obey. What was Damien doing out in public laughing and smiling with another woman?

"What are you looking at?"

"Nothing." Natasha forced her eyes off of Damien and his companion. "I was just surveying the room."

"Is it the couple sitting by the plants?" Nicole's eyes followed the path her sister's had just taken.

"I don't know what you mean." Natasha took a hasty gulp of her coffee, which scalded her tongue and throat as it went down.

"Tash, is that Damien?"

"Yes." Angry, hurt eyes returned to glance at Damien's smiling face as he stared adoringly at his dinner companion. "That's him."

"He's very handsome." Nicole's curious eyes refocused on her sister's. "Who is that with him?"

That was the million-dollar question she herself wanted answered. Natasha's lips thinned as her eyes were drawn back to Damien and his devastatingly beautiful companion. Just seconds ago, she had been singing his praises to her sister, and now she thought him to be a liar, a cheat and a cad!

"Nicole, are you ready to go?" She stood without waiting for her sister's response.

"Of course," Nicole answered. She rose and followed her out, having to almost run to keep up with her.

Damien's table was some way from the door, so she was

sure they could get out without being detected, which they thankfully did. She angrily brushed away a stray tear from her cheek once they were safely outside.

"Tash, it will be all right." Nicole took a tissue out of her bag and handed it to her.

"I'm so stupid!" She berated herself as the tears continued to fall heedlessly.

"No you're not!" Nicole hotly denied as they waited for a cab to stop. "Go back into the restaurant and confront him."

"I can't, Nicole," she whispered miserably.

"Why not?" Nicole placed a hand on her hip. "You two are involved, aren't you?"

"Yes, but we don't have exclusivity."

She couldn't believe she said that; it was to make herself feel better, but it wasn't working. True, they had never talked about seeing other people, but she had just assumed he wouldn't want to, and she certainly didn't.

"That's bull! You just spent the last ten minutes telling me how crazy you are about him."

"Obviously he doesn't share my feelings."

"Maybe his dinner companion is just a friend."

"Maybe." Natasha didn't sound convinced.

"Will you say something to him in the morning?"

"I don't know." She sighed.

"Want some advice?" Nicole took her hand.

"Please."

"Tell him you saw him tonight. It will eat you alive if you don't."

"You're right about that," she admitted. "But I can't and won't cause a scene at work."

"Well, invite him to dinner and then cause a scene."

She laughed as Nicole intended. "Maybe I will. Hey, don't worry about me. I'm a big girl and I'll be fine." She wished she was as confident as she sounded. "Let's grab a cab."

She walked away so that Nicole wouldn't see the monumental hurt forming in her eyes—echoing that in her heart. What a fool she had been to think she meant anything to Damien. What a fool she had been to ever allow him to mean so much to her.

Chapter 10

After a miserable night of imagining Damien and that unnamed woman doing all sorts of sexual acts, Natasha forced herself to walk into rehearsal the next morning with a blank expression. Naturally, her first sight was Damien's smiling face as he talked with a female ballerina, who was hanging on his every word, further incensing her. He glanced up briefly at her entrance and smiled at her, but she didn't acknowledge him.

She nodded curtly to the other dancers in the room and tried to ignore him. Somehow she remained aloof and professional, despite the fact that she was beyond angry. She hated feeling like this, but she was unable to control the insane jealousy coursing through her veins every time she glanced at Damien.

She made it through the morning rehearsals with uttering only a handful of words. As soon as her friends realized she was not in the talking mood, they stopped trying to engage her. At the lunchtime break, she retreated to her dressing room and prayed for the strength to make it through the afternoon and evening rehearsals; however, if they dragged on the way the morning had, she didn't know how she was going to stand it.

"Natasha, what's wrong with you?"

Damien's voice snapped her head up from its previous position of resting in her hands. She stared at his handsome hide as he entered her dressing room.

"Nothing." She quickly looked away.

"It can't be nothing," he contradicted. He walked farther into her dressing room and closed the door behind him. "You've been distracted all morning."

"I have a lot on my mind." To avoid looking at him, she bent down to tighten the already binding lace of her pink slippers.

"Like what." He leaned against the door and folded his arms across his chest. "What is it?"

"Nothing," she contradicted herself. "I'm just tired. My sister surprised me last night with a visit and we were up late."

She wished he would go away; despite her anger, the pure male scent of him was driving her crazy. Damn him and damn herself for still falling prey to his undeniable magnetism. She just wanted to touch him, to feel his flesh beneath her fingertips and to pull that wonderfully skilled mouth down to hers.

He walked over and kneeled down beside her. "I still don't understand your bad mood."

She forced herself to look at him and sighed to enhance her lie. "Nicole wanted to go out to dinner, and by the time we did that and returned home it was late, and then we talked and talked." She shrugged. "I'm just exhausted."

Why didn't he go away and leave her alone before she

confronted him on his choice of dinner companions, before she made an utter fool of herself? She was fighting with every ounce of restraint she possessed to keep a rein on the angry words that wanted so desperately to burst from her mouth. She was determined not to argue with him here at work.

"I'm sorry you overdid it last night, but I need you to get focused on dancing." He stood and placed his hands on his hips. "Need I remind you the ballet premieres in a few weeks?"

"No, you don't have to remind me." Her spine stiffened at his reprimanding tone. "I'll be fine once rehearsal resumes."

"See to it that you are." He turned to leave, but stopped. "You should get in some practice during your break. I expect a much better performance from you after lunch."

"Yes, sir," she dryly responded.

He raised an eyebrow at her before ordering, "I suggest you get to it and don't be late when rehearsal resumes."

"I won't."

He left and she fought down the urge to pick up something and throw it at the closed door. Even though he didn't owe her anything, she felt betrayed, and for the life of her she couldn't shake that feeling. However, she would be damned if he would have fault with her performance when rehearsal resumed. She was a professional and she would act like it if it killed her. Squaring her shoulders, she opened her door to go search for Erina for some intensive practice, praying hard work would diminish her bad mood.

Once she made it home that night, Natasha considered opening the twelve-year-old bottle of Scotch she had bought her father for Christmas to help her forget the day from hell she had just lived through, but she quickly decided against it. Instead, she cleaned her apartment from top to bottom until it was sparkling. Then, she cleaned out her closet—a task she had been avoiding for months—and finally cleaned the oven and repapered her kitchen shelves.

It took several hours until she had finished her onerous projects. By that time her anger, instead of dissipating, had only increased. Nothing would relieve it except for her confronting Damien—the thing she refused to do. As she had told Nicole last night, they had never talked about being monogamous—though she had certainly expected it; apparently Damien had not.

She walked into the living room and sat down on the sofa with a glass of apple juice instead of alcohol. She smiled mockingly at the amber liquid and brought the glass to her lips, but before she could take a sip, the doorbell rang. Sighing in frustration, she set her drink down and walked over to open the door, revealing the object of her anger and generally dismal mood.

Damien walked uninvited into her apartment. She reluctantly closed the door, walked over and sat back down on the sofa while resisting an impulse to pick up her drink and throw it into his damned handsome face.

"What do you want?" She glared at him unceremoniously, and when he sat down beside her, she stood to walk a few feet away from him.

"Well, hello to you too." He stood, placed a hand on her arm and turned her to face him.

She snatched her arm out of his grasp. "I don't want to be bothered tonight, Damien."

"What's wrong with you?" His eyes narrowed at her sour demeanor and actions.

"Why are you always asking me that?"

"Because you always give me a reason to," he shot back. "Now answer me. What's gotten into you?"

"Nothing."

"Don't give me that, Natasha. Are you angry because I was hard on you today at work?"

"No, of course not." She ran fingers through her hair. "You had every right to be."

"I know that. I wasn't apologizing."

His words and tone rankled her already frayed nerves. "Of course you weren't."

"Do you expect me to?" If she did, she was in for a rude awakening.

"You? Apologize?" He frowned at her sarcasm, and she continued in the same tones. "I won't hold my breath for that to happen."

"I don't know what's the matter with you." His mouth set in determined lines. "But if we have to stand here all night until you explain yourself, that's what we're going to do."

"Do you really want to know what's wrong?" Before he could respond, she shouted, "All right. I'll tell you!"

"I wish you would." He grabbed her shoulders and held her still when she tried to walk away from him. "Come on, let's have it. Spit it out."

She angrily did as he ordered. "Who was that woman you had dinner with last night?"

He arched an eyebrow. "How do you know I had dinner with another woman last night?"

His calmly phrased question incensed her further. How dare he come here and rub his affair in her face and refuse to show even the slightest hint of contrition. She snatched her shoulders out of his light grip.

"Because I saw you," she delivered through clenched teeth.

"Why didn't you come over to the table?"

"Are you insane?" She looked at him as if she thought he was.

"Hardly. What's the big deal?"

"There isn't any," she snapped. "Forget I mentioned it."

"Natasha." He studied her closely. "Do you think I was out on a date?"

"Weren't you?"

A slow smile spread across his face. "Are you jealous?"

"Of course I'm not jealous!"

"No?" Amused eyes sought out her enraged ones.

"No." Natasha's eyes grew angry as Damien's fingers entwined around her upper arm when she tried to move past him. "Let go!"

"Not until you stop acting like a nut."

"How dare you call me a nut." She curled her hands into fists at her sides.

"I didn't," he calmly contradicted. "I said you were acting like one."

"Big difference," she scoffed.

"Will you let me explain?"

"You don't owe me any explanation."

"I know I don't," he quickly agreed.

His arrogance offended her. "Why don't you just go away and leave me alone?"

"No." His monosyllabic denial was firm and resolute.

"Damien, let me go and get out, or I'll scream."

"You might scream—" his lips brushed hers "—but it won't be from fear or anger."

Her quickly indrawn breath and rapidly beating pulse at the base of her neck indicated that he spoke the truth. His nearness was killing her, and though she stubbornly fought to move away from him, she longed to be much closer.

"Go away." She whispered the plea.

"Tasha—" he cupped her beautiful face between his hands "—the woman you saw me with last night is my sister, Marcy."

She immediately stilled. Her mouth dropped open in shock. His hands moved to her shoulders.

"That was your sister?"

"Yes." Still smiling, he shook her slightly. "Did you honestly think I would run so easily and quickly into another woman's arms after being with you?"

"I didn't know what to think." She shrugged helplessly.

He frowned. "Your lack of faith is insulting."

"I'm sorry." She lowered her gaze. "It's just that..."

He placed a hand under her chin, forcing her to meet his gaze. "Just that what?"

"I don't know what my place is in your life, Damien." She admitted what was really eating away at her.

"You're a part of my life. Isn't that enough?"

She bit her lower lip before softly admitting, "It was before I saw you with that woman—your sister."

"Then let it be enough now," he softly ordered. "All you had to do was ask me about Marcy."

She frowned slightly. "That's easy for you to say."

He laughed. "I suppose it is."

He kissed the frown from her mouth. "So, are we good?"

"We're good." She wrapped her arms around his neck and chuckled. "Thank goodness Nicole was with me last night, or I don't know what I might have done."

"You have a foul temper," he chided.

"I do." She traced his bottom lip with her fingers. "So you've been warned."

"I appreciate that." His hands slid down her back.

"What else do you appreciate about me?" She fused her mouth to his for several suspended moments.

"Tasha," he murmured against her mouth when her purposeful fingers moved to his chest and slowly unbuttoned his shirt. His eyes twinkled at her actions. "You excite me terribly."

"Are you excited now?" She spread his shirt apart to caress his smooth, hard brown flesh with agile fingers.

"Very." He nipped at her lips.

"Well, let's see how we can take advantage of that." She pushed against his chest until he fell back onto the sofa.

"Yeah." He grinned mischievously. "Let's."

She followed him down onto the sofa, her soft body shaping to his, and she effectively dammed any more words he might potentially utter with her sweet mouth.

The next two weeks flew by until it was the day before Thanksgiving. Natasha had made plans to be with her family, and though she longed to see them, she hated leaving Damien, if only for a few days. She had tried to keep her feelings for him in check, but she had failed miserably. She cared about him very much, and when they were together she couldn't help but believe he felt the same way about her—at least she prayed he did. She knew she was treading on dangerous ground, but as she had told Nicole weeks ago, she had no defense against the strong feelings Damien so easily elicited within her, and that was the simple, frightening, wonderful truth.

Wednesday night, Damien and Natasha lay with their backs resting against the sofa, side by side on the thick carpeted floor in his penthouse in front of the fireplace.

"What time are you leaving to join your family tomorrow?" She snuggled closer as they watched the fire crackle and dance.

"I'm not." He kissed her hair. "Remember, I told you my parents and sister will be going to my uncle's place in Washington."

"Yes, I remember." She sat up and frowned at him. "I thought you would have changed your mind about joining them. You shouldn't be alone at Thanksgiving."

"I don't mind really." He tried to pull her back against him, but she resisted and he sat up to face her.

"Well, I mind." Her frown quickly changed to a smile. "Come home with me."

"No, I can't intrude on your family."

He was just starting to lay old ghosts to rest and become comfortable with the two of them being an exclusive couple. Meeting her family wasn't a step he was ready to take.

"What intrusion? If there is one thing my family always has enough of, it's food—especially at the holidays."

"Tasha, I appreciate the offer, but…"

She frowned. "Don't want to meet my family?"

"No, it's not that," he quickly contradicted. "It's just…" He shrugged helplessly.

"Does the idea terrify you?"

He laughed at her correct assertion. "No, it doesn't."

"It doesn't?" She eyed him skeptically.

"No, I'd love to meet them, but I have too much work…"

"Damien, I can't go away and leave you here all alone."

He softly chided, "It's only for two days, Tasha."

"Two long, lonely days," she dramatically corrected. "I won't enjoy myself a second knowing you're here by yourself."

"It wouldn't be the first time I've been alone on a holiday."

"But you don't have to be alone for this one." Her fingers caressed his cheek. "Please come with me."

Hell, how could he refuse such a heartfelt plea? Before he had fallen for her, it would have been easy. *Fallen for her?* Damn, when had that happened? *Fallen for her?* There was no use denying it. He had definitely fallen for her; his next question made that crystal clear to him.

"When do we leave?" He surrendered and chuckled as

she flew into his arms, knocking him back until he reclined on the carpeted floor with her on top of him.

"First thing in the morning." She kissed him lingeringly. "Thank you for coming with me."

"Thank you for inviting me." He ran his fingers through her hair.

"You're welcome." She smiled before lowering her mouth back down to his.

Natasha and Damien arrived at her parents' home in Rochester early Thanksgiving morning. As soon as the car stopped, Nicole opened the front door of the red two-story brick house and embraced Natasha and then turned to offer Damien the same type of greeting.

"It's nice to see you again, Damien." Nicole smiled as her sister shot her a warning glance.

"Excuse me, have we met?" He glanced from one to the other of the two sisters as they entered the house.

"Not formally, but I saw you when Tash and I went out to dinner about a couple of weeks ago…"

"Nicole," Natasha warningly interrupted.

"Oh, I see." Damien smiled.

"Damien, this is my mother and father, Linda and Lincoln Carter." Natasha introduced them after she was released from bear hugs.

Both her parents were tall and smiling in welcome. Linda's black hair was pulled back into a neat bun. Lincoln sported a neatly trimmed full beard.

"A pleasure to meet you both," Damien said and smiled warmly.

"And you, Damien." Lincoln shook his hand.

Natasha's mother embraced him in a warm hug. "We're so glad you could join us for the holiday."

"Thank you for allowing me to intrude."

"It's no intrusion," Linda assured. "We're happy to have you."

"Come, Damien, let me show you around." Lincoln patted Damien on the back before guiding him away.

Nicole and Natasha followed their mother into the house and then into the kitchen. "Let me look at you." Linda held Natasha at arm's length. "You're not eating enough."

"Momma—" Natasha smiled tolerantly "—I'm a prima ballerina. I have to maintain a certain weight."

"I won't overstuff you." She wagged a stern finger. "Promise."

"Yes, Momma." Natasha nodded her head in agreement. It was useless to argue with her when it came to food, or anything else for that matter.

"Mmmm." Nicole sniffed the air. "Momma, everything smells wonderful." She walked over to lift the lid off a pot, only to have her hand knocked away by a wooden spoon.

"You will keep out of my pots until the food is ready," she sternly warned her youngest, who could never resist sampling everything.

"Just a little taste." Nicole wasn't sidetracked, taking the spoon from her mother's fingers and dipping into the pot. Her mother's hand graced through Nicole's short locks.

"Do you see what your sister did to her hair?" their mother bemoaned.

Her mother's sorrowful tone nearly made Natasha laugh. Nicole shook her head behind her mother's head and mouthed the word "help."

"Oh please, Momma, not again!" Nicole returned the top to the pan and hugged her shoulders.

"When I look at Tash's beautiful long hair, and then see what you've done…" Linda glanced from one to the other and then apparently choked up.

"It'll grow back," Nicole promised. "If I want it to, Momma. I like it."

"Yes," Natasha chimed in. "Besides, it's very attractive on her, isn't it?"

"I suppose." Linda continued shaking her head sadly before determinedly sniffing and turning her attention to her other daughter. "So, Tash, what is going on between you and Damien?"

"Nothing." She suddenly wished her mother would return her focus to Nicole's haircut. "He's a friend."

"That's not what your sister says."

Natasha's eyes shot to her sister. "Nicole, what have you done?"

Nicole shrugged apologetically, "You know how persistent Momma is when she wants to know something. The second you called saying you were bringing Damien, she started interrogating me."

"I did no such thing." Linda frowned at her youngest. "Now, Tash, if it was Nathan or Nicole, who have always rushed into things without thinking them through, I would be worried. But you've always weighed the pros and cons of every decision you've made. Did you this time?"

"Yes, Momma," she honestly answered.

"Really?" At her daughter's positive nod, some of her apprehension faded. "Is Damien the reason for the twinkle in your eyes?"

Natasha smiled. "He is."

"Then I owe him a big thank-you, and I intend to tell him so."

Natasha's smile fell. "Momma, please don't question him about our relationship."

"Would I do that?" At her daughters' doubtful expressions, she laughed and promised, "I will be the epitome of tact." Linda eyed her daughter shrewdly. "Naturally, as your mother, I'm curious as to Damien's intentions toward you. What kind of mother would I be if I wasn't?"

"Have you heard from Nathan, Momma?" Nicole hoped her interjection would divert her mother's attention and put her back in her sister's good graces.

"That brother of yours." Linda waved her wooden spoon threateningly. "He's off on some government business and can't be reached. He called to say he'll try to make it for Christmas or New Year's."

"I hope he can." Natasha shot a grateful grin to Nicole for temporarily sidetracking their mother.

"He will get an earful from me when he does finally show up," Linda promised.

Natasha and Nicole exchanged knowing glances and smiles as they walked over to hug their mother, much to her delight.

They all sat down around the table for Thanksgiving dinner later that afternoon. They always ate early because Lincoln liked to recline in front of the television and watch football games for the remainder of the day, nibbling on leftovers—a habit their mother had long since tired of trying to break him of.

Damien enjoyed seeing Natasha interacting with her family. Gone was the cool reserve she exhibited at work. She was spontaneous, relaxed, a loving daughter and a devoted sister.

"Mrs. Carter, this food is wonderful," Damien flattered.

"Linda," she smilingly corrected.

"Linda," he acquiesced. "What did you do to this turkey?"

"It's in the marinade—an old family secret, which perhaps Natasha will tell you one day."

"Momma, please." Natasha nearly choked on her food.

"Linda." Lincoln smiled at his wife tolerantly.

"What?" Linda innocently glanced around the table. "I'm just saying…"

"Momma, stop embarrassing Tash and Damien," Nicole came to the rescue.

"Embarrassing?" She turned indignant eyes to their guest. "Did I embarrass you, Damien?"

Damien suppressed a laugh. "No, ma'am."

"You see?" She glanced from her children to her husband, vindicated. "And you, Tash, did your momma embarrass you?"

"I don't want to talk about this anymore." Natasha pretended intense interest in the food on her plate.

"That one, she is just like her father," Linda said.

"And what's wrong with that?" Lincoln wanted to know, causing his wife to blow him a placating kiss.

"She has a temper, Damien," Linda whispered behind her hand.

"Don't I know it." Damien's ready agreement caused everyone to laugh heartily. "Only a few weeks ago…"

"Damien." Natasha shot him a warning look, which silenced him, though he couldn't suppress a chuckle.

"What a hothead." Linda smiled at her mortified daughter affectionately.

"But a gorgeous one, even if she does have a temper," Damien quickly added, eyes twinkling as he glanced at her bent head.

Natasha bit her lip to keep from responding and took a bite of her food, resisting with all her might the urge to poke him in the side with her fork.

Chapter 11

A little after midnight when everyone was sound asleep, Natasha quietly tiptoed along the hallway to avoid floorboards she knew creaked. Feeling somewhat like a thief in the night, she turned the doorknob and quickly went inside and softly closed the door behind her.

Damien was standing by the window, dressed only in a black robe and nothing else if his bare muscled legs were any indication. He turned and smiled at her as she came in.

He was thrilled she had sneaked into his room. He wanted her but had no intention of going to her while they were under her parents' roof. But since she had come to him, how could he refuse?

He smiled at her stern look. "Am I forgiven for my escapades at dinner?"

"I suppose so, seeing how your tales entertained everyone royally."

"I didn't mean to embarrass you."

"Momma did enough of that herself." She placed her hands on her slender hips. "And you were very helpful."

"She's a lovely woman. So is your sister, and your father is the salt of the earth."

"Thank you." Her heart was warmed by his assessment of her family. "They were all taken with you too."

"I was praying you would come to me tonight." His eyes beckoned her, and she slowly erased the distance that separated them. "Tasha, you know you shouldn't be here."

"I know," she whispered.

"I'm glad you are." Hungry eyes lingered over her feminine curves. "I don't think I could have slept a wink tonight without you."

Her fingertips caressed his cheeks. "I couldn't sleep without you."

"What have you done to me?" He wondered out loud against her hair. "I want you so much—all the time."

Maybe it was being home with her family and seeing how well he fit. Maybe it was his heartfelt words that emboldened her; she didn't know. Suddenly, she had to admit what was in her heart. She didn't think a more perfect time would ever present itself.

"I love you, Damien."

She held her breath as she waited for him to say something—anything. Her solemn admission was met with silence—dead, deafening silence. The fingers that had been massaging her back froze. Her head rose from his chest to stare into his purposefully unreadable expression.

His heart leaped in joy at her admission, before cold, unadulterated fear took its place. He wanted to reciprocate, but as always, trepidation of getting hurt as he had so long ago held him back.

"Nothing to say?" She kept her voice light, almost playful, refusing to show how much his silence hurt.

"Tasha, I care about you."

"But?"

"But—" he turned away from the adoration shining from her eyes "—let's not rush things."

"What have we been doing for the past month, Damien?"

He slowly turned to face her again. "Enjoying each other."

An eyebrow arched. "Is that all?"

He looked uncomfortable. "What do you want me to say?"

"The truth," she softly responded.

"The truth is that I care about you." He walked back toward her and placed his hands on her waist. "I don't want another woman. I'm enjoying what we have, and I thought you were too."

He hoped that would be enough for her. It was all he was capable of right now. He wouldn't allow himself to say the words she wanted to hear, although he feared they were there in his heart. He didn't want to hurt her, but he didn't want to be hurt either. He bore physical as well as emotional scars attesting to the dangers of trusting and loving the wrong person.

"I am," she softly assured.

"So can that be enough for now?"

"Yes." She leaned forward and kissed his lips lightly before continuing, "I believe in us, Damien, and I want you to believe too."

His fingers entangled in her silky tresses and pulled her lips back to his. "I believe this," he growled before lifting her effortlessly into his arms and depositing her onto the bed, divesting himself of his robe and following her down.

His hungry mouth and his body covered hers. He caressed her wildly, fiercely, and she reciprocated in turn. Focused hands pulled the gown and robe from her. Lips and hands feasted on her soft, fragrant flesh. She was unable to keep up with the fevered rush of his hands and lips against her, and she gave up trying, but her hands and mouth grew as demanding and aggressive as his.

They both forgot they were in her parents' home, and anyone could hear them as their fervent groans, demands and threats echoed throughout the room while they rolled over the mattress, limbs entangled. With a life of their own, their bodies joined and mated wildly, as they lost themselves in each other until they both reached the airless summit before spiraling back down to their only anchor—each other—as they clung tight and let themselves fall.

"I have to go, Damien." The regretful words were whispered against his chest several hours later after Natasha glanced at the clock, which read a little after 4:00 a.m. "My mother and father get up at the crack of dawn."

"Mmm," he groaned in protest, pulling her up until her face lay beside his on the pillow. His lips lowered to hers, tasting gently, softly caressing.

"Damien, I have to go." Her soft whisper turned to a sigh when his mouth opened warmly over hers.

"I don't want you to go," he replied against her lips, hands gathering her soft, warm body closer. "Stay, just a little longer," he murmured against her ear as he stretched out on top of her.

"Baby, I can't…" Her words were cut short as his body easily entered hers. "Oh, Jesus!"

"Stay," he repeated against her mouth as he began to move. "Stay for a little while."

"For a little while," she surrendered on a sigh of ecstasy.

Her clinging arms and legs held him tight. His mouth dammed her moans of pleasure as he took them flying once again.

* * *

"So how did you sleep?" Nicole's eyes held a twinkle.

"Very well." Natasha sipped her juice. "And you?"

"Not as well as you, I think." Nicole winked at her, placing waffles and bacon onto her own plate.

"Nicole—" she speared a golden waffle with her fork "—what are you hinting at?"

"Nothing." Nicole lowered her voice for her sister's ears only. "I was excited to have you home, so I stopped by your room for a late-night talk, only to find you weren't there."

Natasha's expression remained innocent. "Perhaps I went for a walk."

"Perhaps you went for a ride," Nicole quickly countered, smiling knowingly.

"Actually, I was…" Her voice faded when she was unable to think up a convincing lie.

"Relax, Tash." Nicole winked conspiratorially. "If you hadn't snuck into Damien's room, I would be worried about you."

"If you tell Momma…" She stood and walked over to the coffeepot to fill her cup.

"Tell me what?"

"What she's buying you for Christmas," Nicole smoothly answered. "You're going to love it."

"Not even a little hint?" Linda's eyes brightened.

"No, Momma, you'll have to wait." Natasha kissed her cheek before resuming her seat, silently making a mental note to find her mother something spectacular.

Damien sauntered into the kitchen dressed in black jeans and a black sweatshirt. Natasha somehow resisted an urge to stand up and kiss him passionately. His eyes shifted to her mouth, and she knew he was contemplating doing the same thing.

"Here, Damien, take my seat." Nicole smiled as she moved to the chair across the table from her sister.

"Thanks."

He returned her smile and sat down closely beside Natasha. Their thighs brushed lightly, but it was enough to send intense longing shooting through the core of their beings. They glanced at each other achingly before her mother interrupted.

"Damien, I hope you intend to eat a big breakfast and not be a stingy eater like Natasha." Linda shook her head at the single waffle and sparse scrambled eggs on her plate.

"You can count on me, Mrs. Carter."

To prove his point, he placed waffles, eggs and bacon onto his plate, to her mother's approving smile.

"Good. Enjoy. Enjoy." Linda smiled as she poured him a cup of coffee. "And call me Linda."

"I don't know how you stay as slim as you are with food like this growing up." He rolled his eyes appreciatively as he sampled a piece of waffle, followed by another and another. "Thank you, Linda." He lifted his now-full coffee cup to his mouth.

"Sheer willpower," Natasha confessed.

"Let me know when you want more, Damien," Linda said and smiled.

"I definitely will," he promised, bringing a forkful of eggs to his mouth.

"Momma's mission is to feed the world," Nicole teased.

"You be quiet!" Her mother ruffled her short bangs before shaking her head sadly.

"Oh, Momma, please not again," Nicole and Natasha pleaded in unison, causing Damien to glance at them in confusion.

"She doesn't like Nicole's new haircut," Natasha whispered into his ear.

"Oh, I see." He forced himself not to react to Natasha's nearness. "I think it suits you beautifully."

"Thank you." Nicole absently smoothed her bangs back into place.

"I don't want to talk about it again." Linda turned away from the table frowning and they stifled laughs behind their hands at her obvious angst.

"Good morning, family," her father happily bellowed as he entered the room. He pinched his daughter's cheeks lovingly and slapped Damien on the back as if they were old friends.

"Good morning, sir," Damien responded between mouthfuls.

"None of that sir business. Call me Lincoln. It's good to see a man eat a healthy breakfast." He walked over to kiss his wife, taking a steaming cup of coffee from her before returning and taking his seat at the head of the table.

"You're not going to eat all of that, are you?" Natasha balked as she eyed Damien's full plate.

"Every bite." He crunched down on a piece of bacon.

"Leave the boy alone, Tash," her father scolded. "A man needs good food for energy."

After everyone was seated and had everything they needed, only then did Linda pour herself a cup of coffee and sit down at the opposite end of the table from her husband.

"I see where Natasha and Nicole get their beauty from."

"Thank you, Damien." Linda glanced proudly at her daughters. "They are lovely, aren't they?"

"Very." Damien's eyes lingered on Natasha.

Natasha went purposefully silent for a while as she watched Damien effortlessly interacting with her parents and her sister. Sensing her appraising eyes, he turned to smile at her before turning to answer her father's question.

Her happy eyes connected with Nicole, who smiled at her, winked and secretly gave her a thumbs-up sign.

Damien smiled as he intercepted Nicole's message for her sister and, not the least embarrassed at being caught, she impulsively blew him a kiss. He smiled at her. He surveyed the people around the table. It was a warm and loving home, much like his. Natasha must have been very happy growing up here with siblings and parents who obviously loved each other very much.

Much to his delight, from the moment he had met them, he had known they were down-to-earth, real people who didn't put on airs or try to be something that they weren't. They were his kind of people, so unlike most of the ones he met in his line of business—those who were always thinking of ways to use and get over—and so unlike the cold, unfeeling, viperous people who had raised an equally abhorrent child who had almost single-handedly destroyed his life—Mia.

"Damien, are you ready to go?" Lincoln thankfully interrupted his thoughts, and at his positive nod, they both stood.

"Go where?" The three women echoed together.

"To your father's studio to see some of his art." Damien shoved his arms into his black leather jacket.

"To his studio?" The same trio of voices echoed again.

"Yes. Why so surprised?" Damien glanced into the three sets of wide eyes.

"They will tell you that I'm very protective of my work space." Lincoln shook his head in remonstration at his family. "But don't listen to them. Anyone is welcome there anytime."

"That is a slight exaggeration," his wife reprimanded. "You should consider yourself lucky to enter his private domain."

"I do now."

"Come, you will tell me what you think of my work." Lincoln pinched his daughter's cheek. "And I'll tell you a few secrets about Tash."

"Deal." Damien smiled in anticipation.

"Daddy." Natasha turned warning eyes on him. "You're kidding, I hope."

"I'm definitely ready to go now." Damien laughed.

"Then follow me." Lincoln opened the kitchen door.

"Daddy…" Tasha warned.

"We'll see you women later." He winked at them all before leading Damien out.

"Momma, can't you do something with him?"

"I have tried, Tash." She shook her head ruefully. "But what can be done?"

"Nicole?" She turned pleading eyes on her sister.

"Just pray he doesn't reveal any really embarrassing moments." Nicole patted her shoulder in commiseration.

"You two are a great help."

She glanced worriedly at the closed door. Her mother and sister chuckled. She wondered what secrets her father was revealing and how she was going to withstand dying from embarrassment the next time she saw Damien.

"What's gotten you so upset?"

Natasha's head jerked up from the piano keyboard. "Nothing. I'm not angry."

"I didn't say you were angry." Nicole walked over and leaned against the piano. "You always play this melancholy piece when you're troubled."

"Nicole, I really don't feel like talking."

"Since when has that ever stopped me?" Nicole laughed.

"Never." Natasha's fingers stilled over the ivory-and-black keys.

"Tell me what's wrong, Tash."

She sighed before admitting, "Last night I told Damien I love him."

"And?" Nicole sat beside her on the bench.

"And nothing." Natasha stood and stared out the bay windows. "He did say he cares about me."

"Well, that's far from nothing, Tash," Nicole corrected. "He is a man, and by nature of his gender, he has commitment issues."

"Yes." Natasha smiled slightly. "I suppose that's true."

"Give him some time, Tash," Nicole suggested, adding gently, "If it's meant to be, it will be."

"When did you become so philosophical?"

"I guess I'm mellowing in my old age," Nicole laughed.

"Oh yes, your ripe old age of twenty-four," Natasha scoffed.

"Is he worth waiting for?"

"Yes, he is," she whispered without hesitation.

"Then wait. You want to hear the words from him now, but does it matter if he tells you today or tomorrow, as long as he tells you? You two have all the time in the world to build a wonderful, lasting relationship, so don't rush it."

Natasha smiled slightly. "How did you become so wise?"

"Nathan and I take after Momma. You take after Daddy. Both of you are always too hotheaded to see things logically."

"Thanks!"

"You're welcome. Now stop borrowing trouble." Nicole pulled her in the direction of the kitchen. "Come on, let's go see what Momma is whipping up for lunch."

"Deal." Natasha smiled as they walked off into the kitchen.

The time with her family passed by as it always did, much too quickly. They had been back in Manhattan for two days. After spending their days together at work, neither of them shied away from spending their nights together, either at her place or his, each finding it unbearable to be apart from the other for very long.

"Mmm something smells good." Damien sniffed the air appreciatively as he let himself into her apartment.

"I hope it tastes good." She came out of the kitchen at his voice and kissed him passionately.

"You taste good," he murmured against her lips.

"It's the lasagna." She smiled, biting his chin lightly.

"You made me lasagna?" He was touched she had made his favorite meal.

"Yes, I made it last night, and all I had to do tonight was warm it up and make the salad," she explained. "Go wash up and come to the table," she ordered.

He did as he was told and they sat facing each other at the table, where candles flickered gently and soft, romantic music played in the background.

"I can't believe you went to all this trouble for me."

"Nothing is too much trouble for the man I love."

Her response was quick and without the slightest hesitation, attesting to the veracity of her statement. It humbled him.

"Tasha…"

"That doesn't require a response from you, Damien." She smiled softly.

He returned her smile. "Doesn't it?"

"No." She reached across and took his hand. "Not until you're ready to give one."

"Why are you being so understanding?"

"Because—" she treated him to her most innocent smile "—I am a very understanding person."

He tried to hold back laughter, but it burst forth from

him. Without hesitation, she joined in his good humor. He brought the back of her hand to his lips.

"Tasha, you're too much," he said and chuckled.

"Do you know what else I am?"

"What?"

"Patient."

"Yes, you are," he easily agreed. "And may I say that's an admirable trait."

"You may, indeed. In fact, you may compliment me all you like. I won't complain."

He laughed and so did she. They talked about little inconsequential things as they ate—she concentrating more on her salad than lasagna. He complained to her about things that were still wrong with the ballet and bounced ideas for changes and improvements off her, seeming to really want and value her opinion. They were acting just like a normal, very happy couple, and she loved every second of it.

"Well, how is it?"

She anxiously awaited his reaction. He was on his second helping, but was he just being polite? Had she used too much basil? Not enough oregano?

"Tasha, this is the best lasagna I've ever eaten," he replied between mouthfuls.

"Really?" She eyed him suspiciously. "You're not just saying that?"

"No." He placed the last forkful in his mouth. "It's great."

"Good." She released her breath on an audible sigh. "I was worried."

"Why?" He took a drink of his wine.

"I wanted you to like it," she simply explained.

"It's fabulous." He took her hand and kissed her palm. "What's even better is that after a grueling day at work, you came home and did this for me."

"You just made it all worthwhile."

"I'm glad." He sucked one then two of her fingers into his mouth, eyes twinkling mischievously. "What's for dessert?"

"Ah, dessert." She pushed away from the table and walked over to sit on his lap. "I have something very special planned for dessert."

"Yeah?" He pulled her lower lip into his mouth, sucking on it maddeningly before slowly releasing it. "Can I have it now?"

"Oh yes, as much as you want." Her hands cupped his head and pulled his mouth back to hers.

"Damn," he muttered against her lips.

"What's wrong?" She slid her hand inside his shirt, and his eyes darkened dangerously.

"I wish the table was free."

"There's the floor," she suggested, and laughed in delight when he pulled her down onto it before covering her mouth and body hungrily with his.

The next day at rehearsal, a smile lit up Damien's face when he glanced out into the audience. Natasha followed his gaze and saw two women entering the hall being greeted by Rachel with hugs and kisses. Then three sets of eyes turned to stare at her on the stage, and she knew she was the topic of their hushed conversation.

"Everyone, take a fifteen-minute break," Damien threw over his shoulder before leaving the stage.

Once level with his family, he happily embraced both women in turn. He swung his sister around, making her giggle in delight, then he glanced warningly at Rachel, who simply smiled innocently in return. It was obvious she had been discussing him and Natasha with them. He sighed inwardly; women, did they never get tired of matchmaking?

"We didn't want to interrupt your rehearsal," Margaret began. "But Marcy insisted that we stop by to tell you how much we missed you at Thanksgiving."

Marcy and Damien exchanged knowing looks at their mother's words. He was sure stopping by had been his mother's idea, not Marcy's.

"I missed all of you too, Mom," Damien assured, adding as he glanced toward the stage, eyes lingering on Natasha, who was doing her best not to stare at him, "I wound up having a nice time myself."

"Really?" Marcy didn't miss the look.

"You must tell us all about it." Margaret touched her son's arm, forcing him to refocus his gaze on her. "Who do you keep looking at?"

"No one," Damien denied. "Just keeping an eye on my dancers."

"One in particular," Rachel added under her breath.

"Do tell." Margaret's eyes sparkled with interest. "Which one?"

"The ballerina in the lavender, Natasha Carter." Rachel ignored Damien's darkening countenance. "She's dancing the lead."

"She's very good," Marcy stated after they all watched Natasha and Dennis dance for a few seconds. "And pretty."

"Right on both counts, Marce," Damien agreed on a sigh.

"So you've noticed how pretty she is?" Margaret approved. "What else have you noticed about her?"

"Mom, don't start." He could see the wheels were turning in her head, thanks in large part to his nosy choreographer.

"Don't start what? I'm simply asking a very innocent question."

Damien's eyes narrowed as Rachel suppressed a chuckle. "Rachel, don't you have some work to do?"

"I suppose I could find some." A smile played about her lips.

"Please do," Damien dryly suggested.

"It was lovely seeing you two." Rachel hugged Marcy and Margaret in turn. "We'll have to get together soon."

"Why don't you join us for dinner tonight?" Marcy suggested.

Rachel glanced at Damien before declining. "I have a date tonight, but another time?"

"Definitely, dear," Margaret agreed as Rachel left the trio alone. "Damien, do you have plans for dinner?"

"No, Mom." He sighed. "I'm free."

"Wonderful." Margaret beamed. "Feel free to bring a date."

"Aren't I good enough for you?" Damien teased.

"Of course you are." Margaret glanced at a smiling Marcy. "But if you're seeing someone, she's more than welcome."

"Regardless of what you've been told, Mom—" Damien glanced pointedly at Rachel's retreating back "—I've been far too busy getting the ballet ready to engage in dating."

"Really? That's not exactly what we hear, dear."

"Oh, I'm sure it isn't, but that's the truth." Damien kissed his mother's cheek. "Now, I've got to get back to work."

"Of course, dear." Margaret curbed her curiosity for now. "We'll have a nice long talk tonight, Damien Michael Johnson."

"Okay, Mom," he agreed, sighing inwardly. When she used his full name, he knew he was in for it.

"See you tonight, Dami." Marcy smiled knowingly at him.

"You are no help," he whispered in her ear.

She shrugged at him and, taking their mother's arm, left with a backward wave and a mischievous grin.

* * *

That night Damien sat around the white linen-covered table with his mother and sister. Marcy watched him without saying much, though he instinctively knew she was full of questions he would no doubt be bombarded with soon.

"So, Damien, what's going on with you and Natasha Carter?" his mother questioned.

"Nothing, Mom," he sighed. *Here we go.*

"I'm your mother, dear." Margaret smiled. "You can't fool me."

"Especially not with Rachel acting as your mole," he muttered.

Margaret laughed. "You leave Rachel alone. She only wants to see you happy."

He sighed. "I know, but I can handle my own affairs."

Margaret's expression brightened. "Are you having an affair with Natasha?"

"I like her," he admitted.

"And?" Margaret waited for more information.

"And what?" Damien sipped his wine.

"Are you serious about her? How does she feel about you? Are you thinking long term?" Margaret rattled off a few of her top questions.

"Mom, stop browbeating Dami," Marcy suggested.

"Browbeating?" Margaret balked at her daughter's description. "Damien, was I browbeating you?"

"Yes," Damien dryly agreed, and Marcy laughed.

"Oh, how you two always stick together." Margaret shook her head in exasperation.

"That's how you raised us," they replied in unison and then chuckled as their mother rolled her eyes heavenward.

"If you'll excuse me." Margaret rose and left her frustrating offspring alone.

"Poor Mom, we're going to give her a nervous breakdown if we don't settle down soon." Damien laughed as he watched her walk away toward the ladies' room.

"You first." Marcy smiled sweetly.

"Maybe I'll surprise you." He glanced at his phone to see if he had any messages.

"So, are you involved with Natasha?"

"Not that it's any of your business, my darling little sister, but yes, I am."

"How interesting." March sat back in her seat and smiled like the cat that swallowed the canary, finding out in a few seconds what her mother hadn't accomplished all night.

"What's that smile about?"

"You've never been at a loss for a beautiful woman on your arm."

"No, I haven't."

"But you've never once said you were involved with any of them."

He shrugged. "Just a figure of speech, Marce."

"I don't think so." She watched him closely. "Natasha *is* important to you, isn't she?"

"Marcy—" he covered her hand with his "—I love you very, very much."

"But mind my own business," she finished for him with a smirk.

"Exactly." He brought her hand to his lips.

"Dami, I just want you to enjoy life and be happy." She leaned forward. "You would do the same for me."

"I know." He sighed. "But you wouldn't like it any more than I do."

"That wouldn't stop you."

"No, it wouldn't," he agreed with a chuckle.

"Then I can't let it stop me," she said and laughed. "Now answer my question. Are you serious about Natasha?"

"I could be—if I allow myself to." He paused before admitting, "I want her."

"But the past is holding you back."

"Yes." His eyes clouded. "And you know why."

"I do, but it's time, Dami," she softly declared.

"For what?"

"To take a chance on someone again." She watched him closely. "Is Natasha that person?"

"Maybe." He thoughtfully rubbed his chin. "Maybe she is."

Chapter 12

After dinner with his mother and sister, Damien stopped by Natasha's apartment. When he let himself in, she was sitting on the sofa in a short red robe, reading a book, which she laid on the table at his entrance.

"How was dinner?" She smiled as he sat beside her on the sofa, placing one hand on her bare knee.

"Good." He lifted her hand and kissed her palm. "I missed you."

"I missed you too." She kissed his lips lightly.

He ran his fingers through her hair and smiled when she purred. "I would have invited you, but…"

She placed a finger on his lips. "I understand why you didn't."

"I know you do." He nibbled at her fingers.

The fingers of her free hand traced his brow. "You look tired."

He smiled devilishly. "I'm not that tired."

"Oh, you're not?" She giggled when he bobbed his eyebrows.

"No, ma'am." His mouth lowered to hers.

"Come to bed with me." She avoided his mouth, took his hand and pulled him to his feet.

"I thought you'd never ask."

"I'm not asking—" she pulled him toward the bedroom "—I'm demanding."

"I don't like aggressive women." He frowned in mock indignation as she undid his tie and slid his jacket from his shoulders. His shirt quickly followed.

"We will see about that."

She pushed his shoulders until he fell across the bed. She followed him down, straddling him, undressing him slowly and driving him crazy with butterfly kisses and light caresses, all the while skillfully avoiding his advances. Even when he was almost insane with desire, she continued to sweetly torture him.

"Do you like aggressive women now?" She kissed him deeply and then moved away. "Do you?" She removed her robe and slowly, deliberately brought him inside her.

"Yes!" He hissed the word sitting up, arms going around her, mouth attaching to a breast.

Her slender arms held him close, fingers anchoring fast to his head as he continued to ravage her flesh. He pulled her tight, lifting his head and fusing his mouth to hers as she took him with her for a ride on tumultuous, stormy seas.

Her body expertly milked his. His mouth fastened on her other breast. Her back arched gracefully, sending more of her firm breast into his greedy mouth. Feverish hands roamed across her back to her hips, pulling her tighter when she sought to teasingly withdraw. Hands on his head, she pulled his mouth away from her flesh to fuse hotly with hers. Their tongues made wild love and their bodies fervently mimicked their urgent, passionate dance.

Much too quickly, they shuddered from rapture and gasped out loud before crashing back into the shore, falling against feather-soft pillows nearly unconscious, panting and clinging tightly as their hearts continued beating furiously as one.

A few days later, Natasha leaned over the bathroom sink splashing cold water onto her numb face. After several seconds, she glanced at her horrified reflection in the mirror. This couldn't be happening; not now! She sank down onto the toilet seat and placed a hand to her swimming head while the other shakily brought the small white object into view again. She must have read it wrong, but having performed the test twice, she knew she hadn't.

She had felt a little nauseated for the past week or so and her appetite had increased some, but she had attributed it to the rigors of getting ready for Christmas and putting the final touches on the ballet. Her energy level was still high and she hadn't gained an ounce of weight.

A hand went to her stomach, fingers tracing gingerly across her flat abdomen. The truth hit her like a ton of bricks—according to the test, she was pregnant!

How could she be pregnant? She nearly laughed out loud at the absurdity of that silently posed question—of course she knew *how* she was pregnant, but… Oh, God, what was she going to do? She racked her brain; she and Damien had been very careful to use protection—except…she paused and groaned inwardly—except in Saratoga Springs after her shower when they had fallen into each other's arms. But still, she was on the pill, so why hadn't it worked?

She ran into her bedroom, grabbed her tablet and typed furiously into the search bar and impatiently waited for tons of links to appear. After reading several, she clicked on one—*Five Reasons the Pill Doesn't Work*—and read through each cause listed. She hadn't drunk a lot of alcohol, she hadn't been on antibiotics, she hadn't missed her pill. Her eyes widened as she read the next reason—failing to take the pill at the same time every day.

Oh, Lord! She remembered the morning she had left for Saratoga Springs. She had been rushing around getting ready, and Simone, followed by Dennis, had phoned her while she was packing, and she hadn't taken her pill until after lunch when she normally took it first thing in the morning. It seemed like such a trivial mishap, but it was the only thing she could figure as to why she was in the predicament she now found herself.

She had missed her pill that morning—dammit! That was the only explanation why she had conceived. She placed a hand to her mouth. One time, one time out of many she had forgotten to take her pill on time, and the result was catastrophic. Why oh why hadn't she switched to the patch as Nicole had suggested? If she had, this wouldn't have happened. Oh, God, what was she going to do?

"Tasha, where are you?" Damien's voice rang out from the other room. "Tasha?"

"I'm in the bedroom." She jumped up, ran into the bathroom and hastily threw the pregnancy test in the back corner under the sink. "I'll be right out."

"Okay."

She released her breath on a shaky sigh and took several gulps of air while she tried to calm herself. How was she going to face him? She couldn't do it now—but she had to; he was here and she couldn't hide in the bathroom indefinitely. Taking a ragged breath and releasing it noisily, she dried her damp cheeks, tucked her hair behind her ears and opened the door.

"Hi, baby." He smiled as she entered the living room.

"Hi."

She went into his arms and lifted her mouth for his kiss, which was briefer than intended when he felt her cold lips. He pulled back to stare at her and placed a hand on her clammy cheek.

He frowned. "You don't look well."

"I feel a little sick."

He felt her brow. "Was it something that you ate?"

"I—I don't know." Her fingers clung to his shirtfront. "Maybe."

"Can I get you anything?"

"No." She managed a smile. "I'll be all right."

He touched her forehead with the back of his hand. "I hope you're not coming down with something."

"I'm sure I'm not," she reassured as Damien led her to the sofa and pulled her into his arms. "I'll be fine."

"I'll make sure you are." He stroked her back. "I'll take care of you."

"Will you?" she mumbled against his chest.

"Of course." He pulled her closer. "Just relax, baby."

She clung to him, wondering if his words were true. Would he take care of her once he knew she was having his baby, or would he run fast in the other direction? What was she herself going to do about this completely unexpected situation that threatened to sidetrack her career?

How was she going to tell the love of her life she was pregnant when he hadn't even told her he loved her yet? She closed her eyes tightly and clung to him as a wave of pure unadulterated fear assailed her. What was she going to do?

The next morning Natasha made it to rehearsal at her usual time. Once she reached the safety of her dressing room, she dropped her gym bag and coat over a chair and walked warily toward the floor-to-ceiling mirrors. She pulled up her black sweater and placed wary fingers on her flat stomach. She watched in the mirror as her fingers traveled lightly over the smooth brown skin. She looked the same as she had yesterday, the day before and the day before that, but she was different—she might not look physically different, but she was. She was going to be a mother.

"Tasha?"

At the sound of Damien's voice, she yanked her sweater down and plopped into a chair seconds before he walked into her dressing room.

Natasha managed a smile. "Good morning."

"How are you feeling?"

"I'm fine." She took off her boots and placed on her ballerina slippers. "Really."

"You don't look fine." He placed a hand under her chin and inspected her pale complexion.

"Thanks!" She snatched her chin away in irritation and stood.

"What's wrong?" He touched her arm, pulling her around to face him. "I'm only concerned about you."

"I don't need you to be concerned about me." She sighed in irritation. "I'm fine."

She really didn't want to be angry with him. She knew he was worried about her, but she had enough on her mind and her nerves were frayed to breaking. She needed to think and not be hounded by him of all people—not now.

"Are you?"

"Yes," she screamed and ran frustrated fingers through her loose hair. "What do I have to do to convince you?"

"For one thing—" his nostrils flared "—you can stop shouting at me."

"I will—" she placed her hands on her hips "—if you stop badgering me!"

"Fine!" His lips thinned. "Don't be late for rehearsal," he icily ordered and stormed out, slamming the door behind him.

She slowly walked to the door to call him back and apologize, but she stopped herself and sat down instead. She didn't know what she would say to him to explain her short temper except tell him the truth, and she wasn't ready to do that right now. First, she had to come to grips with her condition and the drastic changes a child would necessitate in her life for herself. Secondly, trying to anticipate his reaction scared her to death—one moment, she thought he would be happy, and the other, she was certain he would feel trapped.

Her shoulders stiffened when a soft knock sounded on her door. It couldn't be Damien again, could it? No, he wouldn't knock so softly—especially not after his heated exit a few seconds ago.

"Come in."

Rachel opened the door and peaked inside. "Are you okay, Natasha?"

"Oh, for goodness' sake!" She raised her eyes heavenward. "I am so tired of people asking me that!" Realizing she was shouting, she lowered her voice. "I'm sorry, Rachel, but I'm fine."

"Okay." Rachel didn't look at all convinced. "It's just that I ran into Damien—actually, he nearly knocked me over," she amended.

"We had a little…misunderstanding." She avoided Rachel's eyes.

"Is that all?"

"Yes, we'll straighten it out later." She sat back down in her chair. "I need to finish getting ready."

"Okay, but if you need to talk…"

"I know where to find you." Natasha sighed and looked up to encounter sympathetic eyes. "Rachel?"

"Yes?"

"Thanks." She smiled more genuinely this time.

"No problem." Rachel returned her smile. "I think I'd better go and find Damien before he bites someone's head off—literally." She chuckled before leaving.

Natasha thought that sounded like an excellent idea; he was in an extraordinarily foul temper—made so by her unexplained, moody behavior. Sighing, she cradled her aching head in her hands and willed herself to get ready for the long day ahead.

Damien sighed inwardly for what seemed like the fiftieth time this morning. Natasha was in the midst of the worst rehearsal performance he had ever seen her give. He was trying to curb his criticism because, despite her denials, he knew she wasn't feeling well, but he had to say something—everyone would wonder if he didn't.

"Natasha—" he motioned for the music to stop. "Your performance is simply unacceptable."

She bit her lower lip. "I'm sorry."

"Try it again."

"Yes, sir."

She danced again and stopped when Damien quickly held up his hand, halting the orchestra once more. She glanced at Erina, who was also frowning at her and Natasha knew she wouldn't get any sympathy from her coach—and frankly she didn't deserve any.

"What is the matter?" Damien frowned.

Natasha knew he was being kinder than he should. She was dancing horrendously—she and everyone else knew it. Her mind wasn't on the steps to the ballet, but rather on her unexpected physical state, her pregnancy—that and her argument with Damien this morning was all she seemed capable of thinking about.

"Natasha!"

She jumped at Damien's sharp calling of her name and squared her shoulders, inhaling and exhaling slowly before lifting her eyes to his, in which she saw a mixture of concern and frustration.

"Sir?"

"Don't sir me." He quickly ascended the stairs to the stage. "What is the matter with you today?"

"I—don't know."

"Well, I need you to find out before we resume rehearsals," he tightly ordered and then turned to address the other dancers. "Let's break for lunch and meet back in an hour and a half."

With that, he left the stage without another word to her. Natasha followed his lead and went directly to her dressing room without talking to a soul. She had no sooner made it to her private sanctuary and sat down before Damien walked through the door, closing it pointedly behind him.

"Natasha, are you still feeling ill?"

"No, I feel fine." She sighed.

"Then what's wrong?" He sat down beside her. "I've never seen you dance as poorly as you did this morning."

"I'm just having an off day." She winced at his criticism. "I have a lot on my mind."

He placed a hand on her knee. "Share it with me."

Part of her wanted to, part of her was terrified to. He was being so kind and concerned, and she would like nothing better than to fall into his arms and let him make everything all right; but she couldn't—he couldn't. She had to come to grips with her situation herself before she could deal with his reactions—whatever they were going to be. She needed some time to herself now more than ever.

"Damien." She stood and placed a little distance between them. "I need a break."

He frowned and also stood. "Do you want to go home?"

"No." She placed a hand to her aching head. "You don't understand."

"Help me to."

She stared at him silently for a few seconds before admitting, "I need a break from us."

His eyebrow rose. "From us?"

"Yes, from our personal relationship."

"Why?"

"Because." She shrugged. "I just need it."

"That's not an explanation, Natasha."

"It's not one you want to hear," she corrected. "Look, I just need some time alone."

"Are you angry with me for some reason?"

"No." She forced herself to gaze into his confused eyes. "Not at all."

"Then I don't understand. We were fine last night, and this morning out of the blue you decide you need a break?"

"Yes."

"Natasha." The way he sighed her name conveyed his frustration. "This doesn't make any sense."

"I'm sorry."

"I don't want your apology." He slowly enunciated his next words. "I want to know what's wrong with you."

"For goodness' sake, I don't want to see you for a while. Don't I have the right to choose who I do and don't want to spend my free time with?" She paused before verbalizing her next hurtful words. "On top of everything else, do I have to worry about my job being in jeopardy because I need a break from us?"

His eyes darkened dangerously. His hands slowly balled

into tight fists, and he silently counted to ten before he answered her distasteful question.

"Have I *ever* made you feel as if you owed me *anything* for your job—except hard work and a flawless performance?"

"No," she softly admitted.

"Then why the hell would you ask me that?"

She flinched at his justified rage. "The way you're behaving, I just wondered."

"The way I'm behaving? Natasha…" He took a deep breath and released it noisily. "Fine, if this is what you want, you've got it." He angrily walked out the door before he said something he would regret.

Coming to a decision, Natasha picked up her phone and dialed the one person who could help her. She had to do something before she completely alienated the man she loved and every friend she had. She impatiently tapped her fingers on the tabletop while she waited for the phone to be answered.

"Nicole?" Natasha's voice was strained. "No, I'm not fine at all. I know it's short notice, but could you come into Manhattan tonight and sleep over?" She listened and then assured, "I just need to talk to you about something important. I need your wise advice, and please don't tell Mom and Dad anything is going on with me. Okay?"

They agreed to meet after rehearsal that night. After she hung up the phone, Natasha prayed for strength to make it through the long hours that remained until this horrendous day would be over.

The remainder of the day was like working in a dynamite factory—everyone was afraid to breathe for fear of igniting a devastating explosion in Damien, who made no pretense of the fact that he was royally pissed. When quitting time came, they all cleared out of the building in record time, especially Natasha. When she arrived home, thankfully Nicole was waiting for her in the lobby.

Nicole took one look at her sister's strained face and pulled her into her arms. "Tash, what's wrong?"

"Oh, Nicole." Natasha held her close again. "I'm so glad you're here."

"From the looks of you, I should have come sooner." She pulled back and stared at her sad eyes and stressed features. "What is it?"

"Let's go upstairs first." Natasha led her to the elevator, and they didn't speak again until they were seated on her sofa in her apartment.

"Now, tell me." Nicole took both her hands and squeezed comfortingly.

"I don't know where to begin."

"Just say it, Tash. You don't have to prepare me for anything. You know that."

Taking a deep breath, she took her advice and blurted out, "I'm pregnant."

Nicole's mouth dropped wide open. "What?"

"I'm pregnant," Natasha repeated, a little calmer this time.

"Oh, Tash." Nicole smiled and then frowned. "Are you happy about it?"

"Yes," she answered without hesitation. "But I'm also terrified, shocked and frustrated. This is so completely unexpected and…"

"And you haven't told Damien," Nicole finished for her.

"No." Her fingers tightened in her sister's. "What am I going to do?"

"Tash, you have to tell him," Nicole urged and then asked in a whisper, "Are you going to keep the baby?"

"Yes, of course," she quickly reassured. "I couldn't live with myself if I had an abortion."

"Is guilt the only reason you're not considering terminating the pregnancy?"

"No." She gingerly touched her stomach. "I'm terrified. I don't know what this will do to my career or my relationship with Damien. But, Nicole, a life is growing inside me," she concluded in wonder. "It's not the best time, and part of me wishes I wasn't pregnant, but I am, and how can I not want our baby?"

"And you think Damien won't?"

"I honestly don't know. I know he cares about me." Natasha sighed heavily. "But he still hasn't said he loves me, and I need to hear those words before I tell him about the baby, because I don't want him to think I'm using my condition to coerce a confession of love out of him. I don't want him to think I planned this—that I'm trying to trap him."

"He won't think that, Tash."

"How can you be so sure?"

"Because you've told me what he means to you. I've seen how you've changed because of him, and having seen you two together, I know in my heart you and Damien are meant to be."

Natasha chewed her lower lip. "I hope so."

"Believe it," Nicole urged. "Now bounce some pros and cons off me."

"All right." Natasha took a deep breath and began. "My career is definitely a big con. It's finally taking off in the right direction, and a baby will change all that. I'll have to stop dancing eventually. The ballet is scheduled for a five-week run, and I should be able to complete that without problems. Even if it's held over, I'm hopeful that I'll be able to finish my commitment."

"But new projects will have to be put on hold."

"Yes. Oh, Nicole, everything is so uncertain. When will I start to show? Will my energy be sapped? How long will I be able to perform?" She squeezed her sister's hands. "Why did I have to get pregnant *now*? I love Damien. I do. Having his baby isn't an unpleasant reality, but the timing simply sucks."

Nicole squeezed her hands reassuringly. "That's just life, Tash. The more you try to plan, the more the universe throws unexpected curves your way that make you reevaluate everything."

Despite her angst, Natasha smiled. "Are you sure you didn't major in philosophy instead of fashion design?"

"You know I'm a pragmatist." Nicole chuckled. "Now give me another con."

"That's not hard—what do I know about being a mother?"

Nicole laughed. "More than you realize, and what you don't know you'll learn, just as millions of mothers before you have."

"I suppose," Natasha tentatively agreed. "What about Damien? I don't know how to tell him, and I'm terrified he'll blame me for getting pregnant."

"First, you simply have to tell him, because he deserves to know," Nicole calmly informed. "Second, it takes two to make a baby—you both share the responsibility."

"You're right, but I told him I was on the pill, and I forgot to take it on time—that one little mishap resulted in my becoming pregnant. I still can't believe that. How could I *forget* to take my pill on time? I never forget anything. What if he thinks I did it on purpose?"

"Did you make him forget to wear a condom?"

Natasha blushed at Nicole's blunt question. "No."

"Then, case closed," Nicole quickly dismissed. "Any more cons?"

Natasha shook her head. "I've listed the major ones."

"Then give me some pros."

"There's a little life growing inside of me that Damien and I made." Natasha smiled wonderingly and touched her stomach. "Despite everything, I love him already."

Nicole shared her smile. "I'm going to be an aunt."

"Yes, and Mom, Dad and Damien's parents are going to be grandparents," Natasha added. "This baby will be surrounded by love."

"He or she will."

"Damien will be a wonderful father." Natasha's smile blossomed. "I can just see him teaching the baby to skate and ride a horse and play ball. He'll spoil him rotten." She laughed.

"So will his mother," Nicole predicted.

"Of course I will," Natasha promised with a laugh.

"And when you and Damien need a break, you'll have no shortage of volunteers for babysitting duties."

"Can't you see Momma loading me down with baby food recipes?"

"And Daddy will want to paint hundreds of portraits of his grandchild."

They shared a good laugh over the fuss their parents would undoubtedly make over their first grandchild. In a few seconds, tears of happiness were running down Natasha's cheeks.

"Well, I think the pros far outweigh the cons," Nicole judged. "What do you think?"

"I think I'm very lucky to have such a great sister. Thank you for coming, Nicole. I feel so much better talking things over with to you face-to-face."

"You're welcome. I can stay as long as you need me to."

"Can you go into rehearsal for me tomorrow?" Natasha half joked.

Nicole laughed. "I could, but if you value your job, I wouldn't recommend it." She paused before asking, "Are you so afraid of seeing Damien?"

"Yes, but only because I hurt him so today, Nicole. I know I did, but I couldn't help it. I was just so overwhelmed—I still am. I still have a lot to think about, but I don't want to lose Damien—of that I'm certain."

"You won't." Nicole pulled her into a comforting hug. "Damien will be there when you're ready to talk to him. Everything will work out the way it's meant to, Tash."

"I hope so."

Natasha silently prayed her sister was correct; however, why when everything was at long last going so right, had the rug been unceremoniously yanked out from under her feet? The universe, it seemed, had a cruel sense of irony.

Chapter 13

Damien stared out the glass balcony doors, which had become a nightly ritual during the past week, twirling an untasted glass of bourbon in his hands; the amber liquid sloshed haphazardly against the sides, threatening to spill on the polished wood floor. He and Natasha had spoken very little during the past week, except relating to work. Her performance was back to excellent levels, and he supposed she was right. She just needed some time away from him—a fact that still irked him.

He turned toward the elevator as he waited for his unwelcome visitor to arrive. He had been tempted to tell her to go away, but she would just keep coming back, so he'd get it over and be done with it now.

"Damien, what's going on?" Rachel cut to the chase as she stepped off the elevator into his penthouse.

"Hi, Rachel, how are you?"

"I'm fine." Rachel refused to be put off by his sarcasm, "It's you I'm worried about."

"Well, you shouldn't be. I'm good."

"You are not." She placed her hands on her hips. "You've been an absolute terror since you and Natasha stopped seeing each other." Her hand rose to stay his response. "And please, no more denials that you and Natasha have been intimate. I give you kudos. You two have behaved flawlessly and appropriately in public, but anyone who really *knows* you—like me—has noticed the change in your relationship since Saratoga Springs."

"Since you know everything—" he finally tasted his drink "—what do you want from me?"

"I want to know what's gone wrong." She paused and clarified, "Why have you two broken up?"

"Hell if I know. She said she needed some space." He rubbed the perpetual knot of tension in his neck. "I can't figure her out these days. At Thanksgiving, she told me she loved me, and a few weeks later, she needs some space."

"And what did you say when she confessed her feelings?"

"That I care about her."

Rachel's eyebrow rose. "Is that all?"

"What else was I supposed to say?" At her chastising stare, he defensively added, "Look, I'm not going to be pressured into admitting anything."

Rachel placed a hand on her hip. "Did Natasha pressure you?"

"No," he admitted on a sigh. "Actually, she was great about it, although I'm sure my lack of reciprocation upset her."

"Do you think she fabricated this breakup to get you to tell her what she wants to hear?"

"No, Natasha doesn't play games like that. It's one of the things I admire about her."

Rachel smiled. "What else do you admire about her?"

"Rachel, don't start."

She ignored his warning. "How do you feel about her, Damien?"

"I care about her," he reiterated.

"Is that all?" She placed a hand on his arm. "Really?"

"Rachel…"

"Damien, I was worried when I realized you two were becoming an item—albeit a secret item—but in the past few months, I've seen the old Damien I sadly thought was gone reemerge, and that's because of Natasha. Don't lose your one chance at happiness because you're clinging to the past hurts."

"I'm trying to give her what she says she needs."

"What about what you need?" When he didn't respond, she urged, "Go talk to her—I dare you."

An eyebrow rose at her challenge, and she laughed. After several seconds, he joined her. Actually, he felt better than he had since Natasha had unexpectedly kicked him out of her life.

"Maybe I will."

"Do it, or I'll sick Margaret and Marcy on you," she promised with a smile.

"And if you do, you'll be looking for a new job," he threatened.

"You don't scare me, mister," Rachel scoffed. "Now go and take care of your business."

"Good night, Rachel." He kissed her cheek and shepherded her toward the elevator.

"Make it a really good night by going to see Natasha," she suggested before the elevator closed.

Damien stood there for a few seconds before coming to a decision. Reaching for his jacket and picking up his keys, he waited impatiently for the elevator to return.

* * *

Natasha and Damien stared at each other uneasily for a few seconds after she opened the door to her apartment. God, she had missed him over the past week, during which time she had done a lot of thinking and soul-searching, but she still didn't know how to tell him that she was pregnant, and seeing him on her doorstep was sending her into a tailspin.

"Damien, what are you doing here?"

"Aren't you glad to see me?"

"Yes, I am," she softly admitted. "But I thought you were going to give me some space."

"I've given you enough space, Natasha." He took off his jacket and tossed it over a chair. "We need to talk."

"About what?"

"Us."

"What about us?"

He sighed and took her hand. "Tasha, come sit down with me."

"I really should get dinner…"

"Dinner can wait." He pulled her over to the sofa. "Please."

"Okay." She sat down next to him.

"I think I know why you've been upset and distant."

No, you really couldn't. If you did, you'd probably run out that door and never return.

"I've just got a lot on my mind, Damien."

"I know I haven't been fair to you," he continued as if she hadn't spoken.

She frowned. "What are you talking about?"

"You poured your heart out to me at Thanksgiving, and I haven't reciprocated."

"Damien, that isn't what this is about. I don't want you to admit anything you don't feel."

But God, if there was ever a time for you to tell me that you love me, this is it. Was he about to do that? She prayed he was; it would make things so much easier if he did.

"I think it is," he contradicted. "I want you to understand why it's so hard for me to admit my feelings for you—and I do have feelings for you, Tasha, you know that, don't you?"

"Yes." She touched his hand. "I do."

He was silent for a while before admitting, "It happened ten years ago when I was twenty-two—young and stupid." He laughed without humor.

She blinked. "What happened?"

"There was this ballerina, Mia." He began a story he had vowed never to recount again.

"Mia?" she softly repeated.

"We met when I was dancing in a troupe in Atlanta. We started a relationship—one that nearly cost me my life and my career."

Her eyes grew wide. "What happened?"

"I was in love with her—with whom I thought she was," he quickly amended. "She was very good at pretending to be whatever anyone wanted her to be. I soon found out that everything that I fell in love with was a lie." He paused before continuing, "Mia was a gold digger. I was a struggling dancer, but she found out my family was rich—so she set her sights on me. I was her ticket to the good life. Her M.O. was to gain access to the personnel records of dancers she deemed worthy candidates to sink her claws into. She studied her victims' habits, likes, dislikes, views on life—any and everything she could learn about them, and then set about making them believe she was tailor-made for them. Believe me, she was very convincing."

"How many men did she do this to?"

"As far as I know, I was her second mark. The first guy left town to get away from her. Unfortunately, I learned of her plans after I had become entangled in her web of deceit." He laughed self-derisively. "What a fool I was to trust her. I thought she was too good to be true, and she was." He paused to gather his thoughts and continued, "Things were great between us for a few months, but then I started noticing things—her sudden and extreme mood swings, her obsessive jealousy and her dangerously volatile temper. I realized she wasn't who I thought she was and definitely wasn't someone I wanted in my life. I spoke with Rachel, whom I had met several months earlier when I moved to Atlanta. We had hit it off immediately and became friends. She confirmed my assessment of Mia, and I ended the relationship."

"And she accepted your decision?"

"No." He shook his head. "She didn't. I learned what vindictive meant from her."

"What did she do?"

"What didn't she do?" His eyes grew hard. "She showed up unannounced, made scenes at work and in public. Slashed my tires and broke into my apartment." He rattled off the list of offenses.

"That must have been horrible for you."

"It was," he agreed, rubbing his jaw. "This went on for weeks, and as a last resort to keep me, she told me she was pregnant. I was going to marry her until I thankfully found out she was lying about the baby." He closed his eyes briefly. "Thank God I found out in time."

Natasha's heart sank at his words. How ironic was it that she needed to tell him she was pregnant, and he was now confessing that a past girlfriend had tried to trap him with a fake pregnancy? Why did he have to tell her this now, of all times?

"How could she lie about something like that?"

"That was just Mia. She wasn't above saying anything

to get what she wanted." He shrugged. "She really started stalking me after that, and nothing stopped her until one fateful day when I got into a car with her. She promised if I just talked to her, gave her a chance for some closure, she would leave me alone. I was willing to try anything to get her out of my life, so I did as she asked."

"What did she say to you?"

"Not much really. It's what she did that forever changed both of our lives." He paused and she remained silent, giving him the chance to collect his thoughts. "She started driving erratically and said if she couldn't have me, no one would. I demanded she stop the car. She refused, so I wrestled with her for control, and she deliberately crashed us into a concrete wall. She was killed. I was seriously injured and as a result, I went through intensive rehabilitation and I couldn't perform professionally anymore."

"Oh God, Damien." She placed a comforting hand on his arm. "That's the source of your scars, isn't it?"

"Yes," he admitted. "I was very bitter and I don't like thinking about it."

"I understand. You had a right to be bitter."

"I know." He sighed. "But I was destroying myself with hate and rage. My family came down to Atlanta and, along with Rachel, they nursed me back to health through multiple skin grafts and surgeries. They were my lifeline."

"Thank God you had them." She cupped his cheek.

"Yes." He covered her hand with his. "Marcy and my parents persuaded me to come home to New York to fully recuperate and suggested I try choreography instead of performing. Eventually I did, and soon after I founded my ballet company."

"You made a wise move."

"It didn't feel like it at the time, but it was the right choice for me. When my body healed, I realized I was more fueled by choreography, management and direction rather than actually performing. So everything worked out as it was meant to." He covered her hand with his. "But since that ordeal with Mia, I've shunned serious relationships—especially with ballerinas. I've had affairs and I've been photographed with beautiful women on my arms, but I was never serious about any of them." He gazed deeply into her eyes. "When I met you, for the first time I wanted to forget my resolve not to get involved again."

She smiled slightly. "You did?"

"Yes." He kissed her palm. "You have allowed me to trust again, Tasha."

"I'm glad." She kissed him softly before asking, "Why are you telling me this now?"

"Because you deserve to know." He paused. "Because I want you to understand why it's so hard for me to admit what I feel."

"I do understand now." She covered his hand with hers.

"Natasha, I do…"

"No, Damien." She placed a silencing finger on his lips. "You don't owe me any declarations—not out of some sense of duty or because you think it's what I want to hear."

"You are a remarkable woman, do you know that?"

"Just as long as you know it." She smiled when he laughed as she intended.

He pulled her close. "Trust me, I know it."

"I'm glad you told me about Mia."

"So am I." He pulled her closer. "I should have told you sooner. I'm sorry I didn't."

"It's okay. I know now."

Part of her wished he hadn't confessed about Mia right now—not when she was trying to garner the nerve to tell him he was going to be a father. She did understand his reluctance to open up to her better now, but it also made her current predicament that much harder to resolve.

She buried her face in his neck, glad he couldn't see the worry etched across her features. Would he be happy about her pregnancy, or would he believe, like Mia, she was trying to trap him with a child?

"I do care about you," he whispered against her hair. "So much."

"I know you do." She kissed his neck.

After several minutes of silence, he asked, "Haven't you had enough time alone to think?"

"Yeah, I think I have," she agreed.

His arms tightened around her and she hugged him back. He had given her an opening to confess her pregnancy, yet she didn't take it. She was still holding out, hoping with all her heart that one day soon, he would say the three little words she longed to hear, which would give her the courage and reassurance she needed to tell him about their baby.

She still had some fears and uncertainty to deal with, including the confession Damien had just made, but one thing was certain—she wanted Damien in her life, and she wanted their baby. She had to believe he would want them both once she found the courage to confess to him.

The next two weeks since their happy reconciliation flew by. Natasha had mostly come to terms with her unplanned pregnancy, though she was still terrified of the uncertainty it created. Finally she realized there was nothing to be done, except deal with the frightening yet wonderful condition she now found herself in. She still hadn't garnered the courage to tell Damien, but she was working on it.

At long last, the ballet was ready. They had their first dress rehearsal on Christmas Eve, before he released the cast for a two-day Christmas break. They both were going to their respective parents for Christmas—she to Rochester and he would be staying in Manhattan.

"I'll miss you, Damien." Natasha took his face between her hands. "Very, very much."

"Me too." His hands rested on her tiny waist.

"You'll find a little something from me under your tree." She caressed his face with her fingertips.

"Tasha, we said we weren't going to buy each other presents," he reminded.

"I know." She smiled. "But I lied."

"Well…" he slowly began. "You'll find something in your suitcase from me too," he confessed.

She laughed and he pulled her close. He had to fight with everything in him to stop himself from begging her to stay. He had just gotten her back and was loathed to let her go even for a short period, but they were only going to be apart for two days, he silently reminded. He could do without her for a couple of days, couldn't he? They both remained silent and reluctantly pulled apart slightly.

"We'll take our presents with us and put them under our parents' trees, but we won't open them until Christmas morning at exactly eight o'clock. That way even though we're not physically together, it'll seem as if we are."

He smiled at her. "It's a deal."

They gazed at each other, as if memorizing every feature to sustain them while they were apart, before their mouths melted together. They kissed and kissed and kissed.

"Merry Christmas," she whispered against his mouth she pushed out of his wonderful arms and hurriedly left before he saw the unshed tears in her eyes.

"Merry Christmas, Tasha," he replied to the empty room, amazed at how much he wanted to run after her.

* * *

Natasha slowly picked up Damien's present to her as it lay under the now-barren tree. She slowly opened the black velvet box and immediately started crying.

"Tash, what's wrong?" Nicole rushed to her side.

She didn't respond but instead lovingly fingered the gold necklace with two interlocking hearts. He was telling her his heart was intertwined with hers inseparably. He had given her his heart.

Nicole and her parents watched as she slowly raised the necklace out of its box. Tears continued to fall as she cradled it in her palm as if it was the most precious thing in the world, and to her it was.

"Is it from Damien?"

Nicole's question was unnecessary. Only a gift from Damien could reduce her sister to uncontrollable tears. All Natasha was capable of doing was nodding.

"You love him?" Her mother's question was rhetorical.

"Yes, with all my heart." Natasha's voice returned as she smiled at her mother through tears.

"He loves you too," her father responded approvingly.

"He does," Nicole confirmed, squeezing her hand.

"I know he does—now," she agreed, handing the necklace to Nicole, who placed it around her neck.

Nicole glanced at their parents to make certain they were engrossed in each other and their presents before she spoke next. To make certain she wasn't overheard, she pulled Natasha a few feet away.

"I think it's time for you tell him about the baby, Tash."

"I think you're right."

Natasha pulled her sister close. She loved her family dearly, but she was secretly counting the seconds until she could leave and be with Damien again.

* * *

Damien sat around the tree with his family, home on Christmas morning opening gifts. He smiled and laughed, yet his heart wasn't in it. He missed Natasha terribly. Marcy handed him the present Natasha had left for him and he slowly opened it. It was a heavy, expensive oval-shaped crystal frame. Within it was an eight-by-ten oval-shaped charcoal drawing showing them as they were now and at various stages of aging—always together, happy and very much in love. He gently fingered her smiling face and realized she was trying to prove to him that she wanted a life with him—that she would always be there beside him, if he would let her.

Marcy watched her brother's expression and knew he was overcome by whatever the gift had been. She gently took the picture from him and smiled lovingly before showing it to their watchful parents.

"What a lovely drawing, don't you think so, Michael?" Margaret tilted the frame so her husband could see it.

"Yes, it is." Michael agreed.

Margaret gasped as she noticed the signature. "Is Natasha's father Lincoln Carter?"

"Yes, he is." Damien smiled down at Natasha's face as the picture was handed back to him.

"*The* Lincoln Carter?" Margaret's tone echoed her awe at the possibility.

"The only one I know of." Damien shrugged.

"My goodness! Lincoln Carter is one of the most renowned artists in the world."

"Oh," Damien, Marcy and Michael replied simultaneously, unimpressed.

"You three!" Margaret shook her head ruefully and received various chuckles from her family. "What do I have to do to get you to appreciate art?"

"Mother, my profession is the arts," Damien dryly reminded.

"Yes, I know, dear, but dance, not artwork. How many times have I pleaded with you three to accompany me to an art gallery?"

"Oh, Mom, please," Marcy and Damien groaned together.

"Your mother's mentioned Natasha, son." Michael quickly changed the subject. "I can't wait to meet her."

"That makes two of us, darling." Margaret glanced pointedly at their son.

"I was thinking about having a get-together with both of our families before the premiere," Damien responded to his mother's not-so-veiled criticism.

"Wonderful idea," Margaret enthused. "We can have it here."

He, Marcy and their father exchanged knowing, resigned smiles. Margaret loved to plan parties—nothing made her happier, except trying to find suitable spouses for her children.

"Sounds great, Mom. I'll invite Natasha when she gets back," he promised. "But let's keep it casual." He stood and walked over to the window, still staring at the picture in his hands.

It would be two days before he and Natasha would be reunited, and that sounded far too long to him; he couldn't wait to see her. He had spoken to her earlier, but he wanted to touch her and hold her close. He smiled as a welcomed idea formed in his mind.

After receiving a call from Damien, Natasha had decided to cut her visit short by a day and come back to New York Christmas night. She couldn't wait to see him another second and was delighted he felt the same way. Her family had been disappointed, but they had been somewhat pacified that she was going home to be with Damien, whom they liked very much.

As soon as the elevator to the penthouse opened, she flung herself into his waiting arms, pressing her lips to his without speaking. He pulled her off her feet as he carried her to the center of the room. They feasted on each other's lips for long, long minutes, lifting their heads long enough to snatch a quick breath before their lips fused again.

"I missed you," she whispered longingly, placing kisses on his face.

"I missed you too." Strong arms still held her feet off the floor. "How was your Christmas morning?"

"Miserable without you." She kissed his lips again.

"So was mine," he confessed, sitting down on the sofa and placing her in his lap. His finger touched her throat, sliding down to finger the necklace resting just above her collarbone, and she shivered at the contact. "Do you like your present?"

"Oh, yes." Her fingers covered his. "I love the symbolism most of all."

"What symbolism?" Seeking, burning fingers moved farther down her soft skin.

"You know what symbolism." She bit his chin lightly.

"I wanted you to know that you're special to me, Tasha," he seriously stated.

"I know." She kissed his neck lingeringly. "Did you like your gift?"

"Very much." His fingers unbuttoned her cardigan. "It's there."

He pointed to the mantelpiece. She removed her eyes from him long enough to smile at the picture she had given him before she returned her attention to him and pulled his

T-shirt over his head and tossed it onto the floor as he took off her sweater.

"Do you understand my symbolism?" Seeking, maddening hands roamed down his chest to rest low on his stomach.

"Yes, I do. My family loved it too," he murmured against her neck. "They can't wait to meet you."

"I would like that." She tilted her head to give him greater access to her flesh, her hands roaming up his bare chest to his shoulders.

"Mom's planning a get-together for both families a couple of days before the premiere," he replied between tastes of her skin, hands moving to unhook her bra.

"Mmm, that sounds great. Let me know when, and we'll all be there." As eager hands cupped her breasts, her words ended on a groan.

"Good." His mouth skimmed along her jaw as his hands slid down her quivering stomach.

"Damien." Her eyes darkened at his touch. "I need to tell you something."

"Tell me later, Tasha."

"Later," she agreed, pulling his lips back to hers as she reclined on the sofa, taking him with her. Then, they dispensed with words and gave each other a proper hello.

Chapter 14

The night of December 29, their families gathered at the Johnsons' home for food and merriment. Natasha was still apprehensive about becoming a mother, but it was a heady experience knowing a life was growing inside her—a little part of her and a little part of Damien.

She had confided in Nicole that she still hadn't told him about the baby, but she had promised that she would, soon; and that was a promise she meant to keep, having decided the perfect moment to tell Damien he was going to be a father was on New Year's Eve after the ballet premiere—a time for fresh, new beginnings.

The party was going beautifully. Nicole and Marcy hit it off famously, talking endlessly about the world of high fashion. Their respective parents were seated on the sofa across the room, talking like lifelong friends.

"Look at our families." Natasha smiled up at Damien.

"Yeah, it's wonderful, isn't it?" He placed his arm around her waist.

"Yes." She sipped her punch. "I wonder what has our mothers so intensely involved."

"I don't think you want to know." He chuckled as his eyes lighted on his mother's avid face. Oh, he could see the wheels turning.

He returned his gaze to Natasha. She looked so beautiful smiling as she watched their parents so lovingly that his heart lurched. Why was he hesitating? Why not admit to her that he loved her? Would there ever be a more perfect time or place than here, in the midst of everyone they loved, to tell her?

"Natasha?"

"Yes?" She refocused smiling eyes on his somewhat anxious face.

"I want to tell you that I…"

"Natasha, come here for a moment please." Her mother's voice halted his words.

"I'll be right there, Momma," she promised before turning her eyes back to him. "What is it, Damien?"

"I—it can wait." He sighed.

"Are you sure?"

"Yes." He smiled. "Go and see what your mother wants."

"Come with me." She took his hand in hers.

"Bring Damien with you," Margaret ordered.

"I think we're about to find out what they were plotting," Damien whispered, and they smiled at each other as they walked over to their parents.

"I'll get it," Marcy spoke as the doorbell rang. "Excuse me, Nicole." She rose and walked into the foyer.

Upon opening the door, for the first time in her life Marcy Johnson was rendered completely speechless by the sight of a man. His hair was close-shaven in a military-style cut; he had chiseled features and a hard physique that his expensive charcoal suit and matching overcoat couldn't hide. His brown eyes were smiling, and for the life of her, she didn't know how she kept her jaw from dropping to the floor.

"Is this the Johnson residence?"

"What?" Marcy blinked rapidly at the sound of his deep, sexy baritone voice.

"Is this the Johnson residence?" he asked again with a slight smile.

"Yes, yes it is." With great effort, she pulled herself out of her stupor. "I'm Marcy Johnson. What can I do for you?"

He silently sucked in his breath at her question. For a second he wondered if she meant that innocent statement literally. If he told her exactly what he wanted her to do to him, she'd no doubt slap his face.

"I'm Nathan Carter. I believe my family is here."

"Yes, they're here."

He chuckled. "May I come in?"

"Of course." She laughed nervously and stepped aside, allowing him access. "I'm sorry."

As he walked by her, he inhaled deeply the exotic fragrance she wore and felt pure lust form in his stomach. He reminded himself he was here to see his family, not to have a fling with Marcy Johnson or anyone else for that matter. However, one glance at her beautiful face and the sight of her dynamite body covered by the sexy black-and-gold pantsuit she wore was enough to make him forget that fact.

"Everyone is in here." She led the way into the drawing room.

"Nathan!" Natasha, Nicole and their parents exclaimed in unison, running over to hug him.

Marcy watched with a smile as Nathan placed an arm

around Natasha and Nicole's waists lifted them easily off the floor. Wow, strong and gorgeous—what a combination.

"How did you know where we were?" Natasha pulled back from another hug.

"Mom and Dad left directions for me." His eyes echoed the love he saw reflected in hers.

"I can't believe all of my children are finally together again." Linda embraced her son and daughters in one gigantic hug before dabbing at her eyes with a handkerchief.

"Oh, Momma, don't cry!" Natasha pleaded.

"It's just her way." Lincoln kissed his wife's cheek. "She'll be fine."

"I'm too happy to properly scold you for being gone so long, Nathan." Linda sniffed back tears, promising, "I'll do it later."

"Yes, Mom." Nathan acknowledged her threat with a smile and kissed her cheek.

His father patted him on the back and then embraced him in a bear hug before he and Linda returned to sit by Damien's parents. Natasha beckoned to Damien, who walked over to take her hand.

"Nathan, this is Damien."

"It's nice to meet you, Nathan." Damien shook his hand.

"And you, Damien." Nathan smiled, noting the way his sister had automatically gone back to his side, and how right she looked there.

"How long will you be here?" Nicole clung to Nathan's arm.

"At least a month." He kissed the tip of her nose.

"A month," Nicole complained, beating Natasha to the punch. "Is that all?"

"Maybe longer." He smiled tolerantly.

Only now being in their midst did he realize that he had missed his family terribly. True, his job was very demanding and very necessary, but still, it had placed a terrible burden on him and his family over the years—one which was becoming almost unbearable for him.

"Well, at least you're here for the ballet." Natasha's smile turned to a giggle as Damien kissed her neck lingeringly.

Nathan smiled at them. "I wouldn't miss it for the world."

"Natasha, Damien, our parents want you two." Marcy's eyes twinkled as she smiled at the embracing couple.

"Again?" they echoed in unison.

"It seems they have special plans where you two are concerned." Marcy laughed as they stared at each other, sighed and walked away.

"I need a refill." Nicole held up her empty glass and walked away.

"Can I get you a drink, Nathan?"

"No, I'm fine."

"Yes, you are." Marcy's appreciative eyes examined him from head to toe.

"Thank you." He subjected her to a thorough investigation of his own. "You're not bad yourself."

"Thanks." She breathlessly accepted his compliment, and a secretive smile turned up the corners of her mouth.

Nathan watched her suspiciously. "What are you thinking?"

"That's for me to know." Her smile transformed into tinkering laughter at his raised eyebrow.

The party lasted until well after 2 a.m. It seemed that no one wanted to see the good times end. It had been an absolute success, everyone feeling as if they had made friends for life.

"Come in," Natasha invited, as she stood aside to allow him entrance into her apartment.

"As much as I would love to, I can't," Damien declined, remaining on the stoop.

"Why not?" She leaned against the door frame.

"Because we both need to rest up for the premiere." He outlined her lips with his finger. "Especially you, my star."

"And we can't do that together," she admitted on a sigh.

"No, we can't." He smiled and then kissed her but pulled back before he went in too deep.

"What were you going to tell me tonight?"

"It can wait."

Her hand curved around his neck. "Tell me."

He hesitated, but for once not out of fear. This wasn't how he wanted to do it. She deserved candlelight, roses, champagne, soft romantic music—the works—and he promised himself she would have all of that and more.

"I'll make it worth the wait."

"You'd better," she relented and pulled his mouth to hers. "Are you sure you won't come in?"

"Stop tempting me."

"All right." Her fingers traced his brow. "These will be the longest two nights of my life."

"Mine too," he promised, stilling her fingers and bring them to his lips. "But after the premiere…"

"You are all mine," she finished for him.

"And you'll be all mine." He kissed her briefly before determinedly walking away.

"Always," she softly promised. "Damien?"

He turned to face her. "Yes?"

She toyed with telling him about the baby, but quickly decided against it. She wouldn't tell him something so important while standing in the hallway! She wanted it to be perfect when she told him he was going to be a father; God, she prayed he would be happy, because second by second she was becoming more and more overjoyed.

He walked back over to her. "Tasha, what's wrong?"

"Nothing." She shook her head and smiled. "I'm just missing you already."

He kissed her. "Me too."

"I'll be miserable without you," she promised against his mouth.

"So will I." He kissed her lingeringly before reluctantly stepping back. "Good night, Tasha."

"Good night."

She smiled and watched him enter the elevator and leave. Hell or high water, she would tell him after the ballet that she was pregnant. It would be the perfect time—the dawning of a new year, and besides, if she didn't do it soon, she would burst. She just prayed he would be as happy as she was.

New Year's Eve dawned bright, cold and sunshiny. The entire day passed in a blur of activity, and nighttime quickly arrived. Natasha was dressed in a wispy knee-length pale pink gown with silver strands running throughout. Her hair was loose but was held away from her face by a pink-and-silver head wrap.

Approximately fifteen minutes before the ballet began she sat in her dressing room in front of the mirror, putting the finishing touches on her heavy stage makeup, concentrating on applying sparkling gold eye shadow. Satisfied with her appearance, she anxiously wrung her hands and breathed deeply. She couldn't believe the moment was finally here. She was so excited!

"Come in." She turned as someone knocked on her dressing room door.

"How are you doing?"

"Damien!" she exclaimed, running into his arms. "I'm a nervous wreck!"

"Why?" He pulled slightly back, not wanting to wrinkle her costume. "You'll be brilliant."

"You think so?"

"I know so." He kissed her lightly so as not to muss her makeup.

"Kiss me, really kiss me. To hell with my makeup," she ordered, winding her arms around his neck and pulling his lips back to hers, a position they stayed at for long, satisfying minutes.

When they parted, she picked up a tissue and wiped away traces of the lipstick from his mouth, making sure she didn't get anything on the impeccable white jacket, shirt and tie of his tuxedo. His pants, in contrast, were midnight black. The gown she would wear after the ballet was a black sleeveless number she hoped would raise Damien's temperature half as much as his attire did hers. Lord, he looked handsome!

"Natasha, I…" He swore softly as a knock on the door interrupted his words.

"Fifteen minutes, Miss Carter," a man yelled.

"I guess I'd better let you finish getting ready." He released her reluctantly. "Break a leg."

"Thank you. Where will you be?"

"In the wings watching you." He winked. "Where else?"

"Good—" her fingers caressed his hair-covered chin "—I need you close."

His eyes darkened seriously. "I'm always close to you, Tasha."

"Oh, Damien." She fought back tears. If only he knew how true his words were.

"Don't cry." He softly touched his lips to hers.

"I won't." She sniffed and then smiled at him.

"Tonight marks the start of a wonderful new year for us," he promised.

"Yes," she agreed.

He wanted to say more and so did she, but both knew now wasn't the time. After the ballet he would finally tell her the words he knew she longed to hear. Kissing her palm lingeringly, he left before he ruined the wonderful surprise he had in store for her when they were finally alone.

A short while later, the lights suddenly dimmed and the audience sat forward expectantly, like children waiting for a treat. Soft strands of music began playing, and slowly the dancers materialized on the stage in preparation for the start of the ballet.

From the wings, Damien jealously watched Dennis dancing seductively with his Natasha. For the first time in a long time, he wished he was still performing. He would give anything to be the one out there now with her. She was so beautiful, perfect, and she was dancing like an angel, flawless, graceful, enthusiastic and with a myriad of emotions. She brought his passion to life as no other dancer could.

He glanced at the audience, who seemed enthralled, before returning his attention to Natasha. A smile lit up his face and remained there throughout the entirety of her performance. After the first act, the curtain closed to exuberant applause. Natasha and Dennis broke apart, and she ran offstage into Damien's waiting arms.

"You were fabulous!" He swung her around in a circle.

"Was I, really?"

"Perfect." He kissed her cheek and placed his arms around her waist.

He walked her to her dressing room. No sooner had the door closed than his body trapped hers against it and he kissed her achingly. His hands ran down her trembling body and hers slid underneath his jacket, pressing into his back as passion grew within them to the point of explosion.

"Tasha," he rasped against her ear before biting into her lobe.

"Damien, I adore you," she urgently whispered before reluctantly stepping away from him.

"Come back here." He decisively reached for her, but she evaded him.

"I have to get ready for the next act." She removed her headdress.

"Sure you don't need any help undressing?" He purposefully walked toward her, hands moving to her shoulders, pulling her top down her arms.

"I would love it, but we would be very late for the next act, if I accepted." She repositioned her top and wisely opened the door.

He leaned over and whispered for her ears only, "We will finish this to both our satisfaction later."

"Promise?" Her eyes gleamed.

"Oh, yes, I guarantee it," he groaned.

She smiled and blew him a kiss as he reluctantly left. With much effort, she tore her thoughts away from Damien and quickly put on her next costume—this one black and white.

Soon she was back onstage, with Damien watching from the wings. All too soon, the last act arrived, and Natasha was dressed in a wispy, ankle-length white sleeveless creation that flowed around her when she moved. Her hair was completely covered by her white feather headdress, and she was absolutely stunning.

This was the fast-paced, acrobatic part of the ballet. Damien's heart stuck in his throat as Natasha made a flying leap and he prayed Dennis would catch her, which of course he did flawlessly. He was in awe just watching her. She was magnificent, perfect—everything he could have asked for and more. God, how he loved her! He couldn't wait to tell her, and he would tonight.

He glanced out at the audience, who was as enthralled by Natasha as he was. A smile lit up his face. She would be in demand after this stunning performance; he was so happy for her that he could hardly contain himself.

The remainder of the ballet flew by until finally the audience sat in silent awe and dismay that it was over. Then they broke out to thunderous applause.

When the curtains opened again, Dennis and Natasha occupied the stage alone, holding hands. Natasha and Dennis lost count of the curtain calls they made. The secondary characters were sent onstage to take their bows, and then Damien and Rachel faced the standing audience's claps and cheers with bright smiles. Then Natasha came back with Damien, who presented her with a huge bouquet of white roses and kissed her cheeks before leaving her alone onstage to take her solo bows.

She had waited forever to experience this feeling and now that it was here, she longed for Damien to be beside her. She glanced at him as he stood in the wings proudly smiling at her, and nothing had ever felt so perfect in her entire life.

Chapter 15

Unfortunately, Natasha and Damien had to wait much longer than they hoped until they could be alone because an after-ballet party was being held in Damien's penthouse. He had invited the entire cast and crew and their families. The penthouse was huge, comprising the entire top floor of the building, yet there were wall-to-wall people.

A long buffet table with everything imaginable lined one side of a wall. Music played in the background and people danced on one side of the room, or where they stood. Everyone was laughing, happy and having a wonderful time.

"Tash, you were wonderful." Nicole enfolded her in a hug, followed by her parents.

"Thank you. Dancing the lead is the best thing that's ever happened to me."

"The best?" her mother teased.

"Well—" Natasha's eyes sought out Damien's across the room "—maybe second best."

"So Damien is more than a friend," her mother teased. "Isn't he?"

"Yes, Mom, he is, but we want to keep our relationship to ourselves for a little while."

"We understand, sweetheart." Lincoln kissed her cheek. "Just be happy."

"I am, very." Natasha smiled.

"Excuse me, everyone. May I steal Natasha away for a few minutes?" Damien placed a possessive arm around Natasha's waist.

"Of course you may," Linda approved.

Natasha allowed herself to be led away to the dance floor, where Damien pulled her into his arms. She closed her eyes as they barely moved to the soft music. She felt his hand tighten on her waist before his fingers slid caressingly up and down her spine. She sighed in contentment, pulling slightly back to stare into his handsome face.

"It has been a wonderful night," she purred.

"Yes, it has, and it will only get better," he promised. "I only wish…"

"What?" She moved closer. "What do you wish?"

"I wish everyone would disappear so that we could be alone."

"So do I," she groaned. "When are they going to go home?"

"They just got here," he ruefully reminded.

"They did, didn't they?" she softly yet urgently groaned.

"I know." Despite the crowd, he kissed her lightly. "Tasha, before I forget to tell you, I want you to know that you made the premiere a personal success for me tonight."

"We made it a success," she corrected. "We're very good together."

"The best." He smiled.

"The best," she echoed.

"Have I told you how beautiful you are?"

"Thank you." She pressed closer to him. "And you are very handsome. You look so good in that tuxedo."

"Oh, yeah?" He smiled.

"Mmm-hmm." She kissed his cheek.

"I want to kiss you." Hungry eyes locked on her mouth. "Really kiss you."

"What are you waiting for?"

He glanced around. "We have a houseful of people."

"So." She moved closer.

"The entire troupe is here, and we have to maintain our cover, remember?"

She sighed. "I forgot. When are they going to leave?"

He laughed. "Not for hours yet, I'm afraid."

"Oh, God," she moaned in agony. "May time fly by on wings," Natasha prayed.

"Amen," Damien agreed and twirled her across the room. "Hey, we've been doing this for months. A few more hours won't kill us."

She smiled wryly. "Wanna bet?"

"We'll survive." He fought the urge to pull her closer. "And when they leave, the fun really starts, but until then…" he suddenly released her a few feet away from the locked balcony. "Wait two minutes and meet me outside."

She laughed. "What?"

"You heard me." He chuckled before unlocking the balcony doors and disappearing inside.

"Damien," she whispered to his retreating back. A smile flirted about her lips as she glanced at the clock. "What do you have planned?"

One minute before midnight, Marcy strategically positioned herself next to Nathan. She reached him just as the group countdown reached zero and white and black balloons, along with colorful streamers, miraculously began raining down on them.

"Happy New Year, Nathan." She could tell her voice startled him as he turned around to face her.

"Happy New Year, Marcy," he echoed.

Lord, she was gorgeous. Why did she have to be so damned beautiful, and why did he have to meet her now? More important, why did he have to be so attracted to her, when he knew there was no way he could act on that attraction?

Instinctively Marcy knew he was about to shake her hand. She shook her head and placed possessive hands on his broad shoulders.

"It's customary to seal that wish with a kiss," she reminded, and before he could react, she pressed her mouth to his.

He told himself it was only going to be a light kiss; however, once his mouth touched hers and those soft, honeyed folds parted so quickly, so easily, he couldn't help diving in. Her lips were quicksand, and he was drowning in them. The hands on her waist pulled her a little closer. One hand moved up to entangle in her luxuriously thick, soft hair, as he had longed to do since meeting her, and he decided to let himself go a little deeper—for a little while longer.

When long minutes later he pushed her slightly away, she was weakly clinging to his lapels, eyes wide with wonder and longing. He reminded himself he couldn't afford any entanglements emotionally, especially not now; Marcy Johnson could quickly become that—if he let her, which was something he must not do.

Natasha snuck out to the heated balcony as Damien had instructed. The glass doors and windows were covered with curtains, affording them complete privacy.

"Right on time." Damien smiled and handed her a flute of champagne before pulling her into his arms.

"On time for what, Mr. Johnson?" Natasha laughed.

"We're ringing in the new year alone without prying eyes watching our every move." Damien kissed her neck lingeringly.

"Oh, I like the sound of that." She wound her free arm around his neck.

"I thought you might." Damien clinked his flute with hers as the crowd inside could be heard counting down from ten. "Happy New Year, Tasha."

"Happy New Year, Damien."

She pretended to sip her champagne to seal the toast and gladly relinquished her glass to Damien, who deposited them both on a nearby table before pulling her completely into his arms.

His mouth slowly lowered toward hers. They both made the slight movement that had their lips caressing. Natasha stood on her tiptoes to reach his mouth, which played with hers softly for a few moments until the control they had exerted all evening snapped and they both surrendered to heaven.

Natasha wound her arms around his neck. The hands on her waist lifted her effortlessly off the floor, bringing her delectable lip closer to his. Their mouths feasted as if devouring a long-denied banquet of life-sustaining food. She moaned against his lips and opened her mouth wider beneath the insistent, wonderful pressure of his.

They tilted their heads to the right and to the left, trying to taste as much of each other as possible from every vantage point possible. He held her effortlessly against his hard body. Her feet dangled in the air. Her arms tightened around his neck when his piercing tongue danced a fierce ballet with hers before stroking the roof of her mouth maddeningly. She moaned in ecstasy, letting him know she would do anything he asked and silently prayed he would ask for everything she had to give. Time was suspended as they savored their private moment for as long as they could.

It was the wee hours of the morning, nearly daybreak, before the party broke up and Natasha and Damien were finally alone. The penthouse was a mess neither of them wanted to face, so they had gone outside in their formal wear to frolic in the freshly fallen snow; a short while later, they returned to the penthouse giggling, damp and happy.

"Whose idea was it to have a snowball fight in twenty-five degree weather?" Natasha asked, taking off her coat and hat.

"Yours," Damien reminded as he divested himself of his jacket.

"Well, I'm paying the price for my impulsiveness now," she promised. "I'm frozen!" She slowly peeled her ice-covered gloves from rigid fingers.

"I know how to cure that." Damien took her cold hand and led her into the bedroom, and then into the bathroom where he proceeded to undress himself and then her.

A few minutes later, they were enfolded by steamy, hot water while reclining at opposite ends of the oblong sunken bathtub. Natasha slid down until the water pooled around her neck, and she sighed in contentment.

"Warm enough now?"

"Almost." She sat up and floated in his direction until she was straddling him.

"What do you have in mind?" he unnecessarily asked, his hands running down her water-slicked skin, feeling her tremor expectantly at his touch.

"This," she whispered, slipping him inside her, shuddering at the blast of heat melting into heat.

"Tasha," he groaned, pulling her close, engulfing her mouth with his.

He released her mouth long seconds later to trail his tongue across her neck and shoulders before focusing on her luscious breasts. Their bodies continued to generate heat comparable to that of the hot water that lapped caressingly around them.

"I love you," she whispered and sought his mouth again, cutting off his confession to the same as passion quickly overwhelmed them both.

Later, lying close in bed, toasty warmth enveloped Natasha's body and heart. She sighed contentedly. This was heaven; she had everything she needed in Damien's arms.

"Tasha?" Damien whispered in her ear, arm tightening around her waist.

"Hmm?" She pressed her back into his stomach.

"I love you."

She gasped, turned around and stared into his serious eyes. "What did you say?"

He smiled at her tenderly. "I love you."

She laughed joyously. "What took you so long to say it?"

"I was waiting for the right moment."

"And this is it?"

"Yes, it feels right to tell you now." He kissed her softly before pulling back to confess, "I had the entire event planned out. I wanted to give you candlelight, roses and champagne…"

"This is perfect."

"Yeah?" He grinned.

"Oh, yes." She returned his smile.

Their lips gravitated together again and they kissed long and deep. Before things got out of hand, she pulled away slightly and placed a staying hand on his chest.

"I have something to tell you too."

"Tell me later."

She sat up and evaded his lips and arms. "I need to tell you now."

"Okay." He propped his back against the pillows, enjoying the view of her naked flesh. "What is it?"

"Damien—" she bit her lower lip "—I don't want you to think…"

"What?" At her serious expression, he sat up to face her. "Tasha, you're scaring me."

"I'm sorry." She ran fingers through her hair. "I don't mean to."

"Baby, just say it." He took her hand comfortingly. "It'll be all right."

"Okay." She inhaled and exhaled loudly before softly confessing, "Babe…I'm pregnant."

He was silent for several deafening seconds. His mouth dropped open in shock. She held her breath, waiting for him to say something, anything.

"What?" he whispered.

"I'm going to have our baby," she rephrased.

He let out a scream of joy and pulled her close. She exhaled loudly, relaxed instantly and returned his embrace. A radiant smile lit up her face.

"Are you serious?" He pulled back to stare at her.

"Yes." She smiled. "Are you happy?"

"Happy?" He shook his head. "No. I'm ecstatic! But how? I thought you were on the pill?"

"I was—I mean I am." She shook her head. "Believe me, I'm shocked too. The only thing I can figure out is that I was late taking my pill the day we first made love. I know that sounds lame, but…"

"Tasha, I believe you, and anyway, all that matters is that you're pregnant." He smiled.

"Really?" At his positive nod, she cupped his face. "I'm so relieved."

He frowned. "Did you think I wouldn't be happy?"

"After you told me about Mia, I was afraid…"

"Tasha, you are nothing like her—you are the love of my life who has given me life and who's going to have our child. I love you with everything I have, and I never want to be parted from you."

"Oh, Damien." She pressed her mouth to his for long seconds.

"How do you feel about the baby?"

"I'm so happy." Tears swam in her eyes.

"Really?" He watched her closely. "Even though you'll have to put dancing on hold in the near future until after the baby is born?"

"Yes. I won't lie to you. That thought terrified me for a short time, which is why I was such a pain a few weeks ago. But, Damien, I love you and our child," she wanted him to know. "Life is full of give and take. You gain something precious and you risk losing something you value, but I'm looking at this as a temporary setback. I can always return to dancing after the baby is born."

"Of course you can," he agreed. "I'll support whatever you decide to do."

"You'd be okay if I wanted to resume my career?"

"Why wouldn't I be?" He brought her palm to his lips.

"How did I get so lucky?" She trailed her fingers across his cheek. "I love you so much."

"I love you too."

He kissed her far too quickly and got out of bed. She watched as he nakedly padded over to the dresser.

"Where are you going?"

"Not far." He smiled over his shoulder. Opening the

drawer, he took out a black velvet box and turned to watch Natasha's eyes grow wide with surprise and happiness.

"Damien." She placed a hand to her mouth. "What is that?"

He opened the box, bent down on one knee beside the bed and took her left hand in his. When her eyes beheld the beautiful five-carat emerald-cut diamond solitaire lying in a bed of black satin, tears fell unheeded.

"God, I love you, Natasha, much more than I ever thought I could love anyone," he began. "I'm sorry it took me so long to tell you how much you mean to me." He placed the ring onto her ringer. "Will you please marry me?"

"Yes, yes I will!"

Her arms reached for him and pulled him back into the bed and into her arms. Their lips met and pressed close to seal her acceptance, and then she rained kisses across his smiling face before her mouth sought his out again.

"How long have you had this?" she asked between kisses.

"A few days. I wanted to give it to you tonight—a perfect start to the new year together."

"It is perfect." She stared at her ring and then kissed him again. "I'm so glad we found each other."

"So am I." His arms pulled her close. "I never knew what love was until I fell in love with you."

"Neither did I—until I met you," she answered with a tender smile that turned into a slight frown. "You don't feel trapped, do you?"

"Tasha, I feel blessed. I have you, the love of my life, and soon our child will be born. I'm where I want to be," he firmly stated, greedily seeking her mouth. "I've been hooked on you since our first dance."

"So have I." Tears of happiness welled in her eyes. "I love you, Damien."

"I love you too, Tasha." He spoke the words that once

had been so hard and now were so easy to say. "I'll never let you go," he spoke against her mouth.

"Promise?" Her breath intermingled with his.

"I swear." He pulled her closer.

"Then I have everything I want," she whispered as his lips rubbed against hers. "Everything I'll ever need."

"So do I, my love."

He pulled her back against the pillows and sealed his vow with the sweetest kiss either of them had ever known—a kiss and a love that made them breathless.

* * * * *

REQUEST YOUR FREE BOOKS!

2 FREE NOVELS
PLUS 2 FREE GIFTS!

KIMANI
ROMANCE

Love's ultimate destination!